Praise for *Her First Pale*

T0028715

"In *Her First Palestinian* Saeed Teebi brilliantly and skilfully evokes the Palestinian diaspora experience, weaving stories of displacement, long-ing, and loss. His characters, drawn with great empathy and insight, are immigrants and refugees, misfits and outsiders, striving to fit in a complex, modern world while carrying the burden of history. Intelligent, original, and bursting with vitality, *Her First Palestinian* is an assured and highly accom-plished debut that will stay with you long after you finish reading."
— Ayelet Tsabari, author of *The Art of Leaving*

"Saeed Teebi is a patient storyteller. He weaves his stories through glimpses of heritage, snippets of immigration, and depth of understanding. In *Her First Palestinian*, Teebi introduces us to complex and endearing characters. They all ring so true; they feel like half siblings or dear cousins. They are never loud or invasive. They are inviting and warm. Almost friendly as they tell you of themselves, their history, and the personal and societal roads they have to take. However, their wound is always internal, hidden under their agency, prosperity, and the most basic human need of them all: belonging."
— Danny Ramadan, author of *The Foghorn Echoes*

"This beautiful collection not only brings to light the varied and sometimes fraught experiences of diasporic Palestinians but does so with masterful storytelling. These stories are rich and deep, with elegant, tragic, or funny twists that will stay in my mind for a long time."
— Farzana Doctor, author of *Seven*

"A gorgeous debut collection of short stories so complex and rich they make me think that Saeed Teebi has been writing for many years."
— Hasan Namir, author of *God in Pink*

"Saeed Teebi's *Her First Palestinian* is a powerful and propulsive debut collection of stories that dramatizes the experiences of the Palestinian diaspora. Compelling and complex characters displaced and removed from their historical homeland negotiate feelings of loss, estrangement, and complicity in Canada. Skillfully written with penetrating insight into the characters' fractured identities, this book reveals a talented new Canadian voice."
—Jury Citation, Danuta Gleed Literary Award

HER FIRST
PALESTINIAN

AND OTHER STORIES

SAEED TEEBI

Published in Canada in 2022 and the USA in 2022 by House of Anansi Press Inc.
houseofanansi.com

House of Anansi Press is committed to protecting our natural environment. This book is made of material from well-managed FSC®-certified forests, recycled materials, and other controlled sources.

House of Anansi Press is a Global Certified Accessible™ (GCA by Benetech) publisher. The ebook version of this book meets stringent accessibility standards and is available to readers with print disabilities.

28 27 26 25 24   3 4 5 6 7

Library and Archives Canada Cataloguing in Publication
Title: Her first Palestinian : and other stories / Saeed Teebi.
Names: Teebi, Saeed, author.
Identifiers: Canadiana (print) 20220203261 | Canadiana (ebook) 20220203423 |
ISBN 9781487010874 (softcover) | ISBN 9781487010881 (EPUB)
Classification: LCC PS8639.E445 H47 2022 | DDC C813/.6—dc23

Cover design: Alysia Shewchuk
Text design and typesetting: Marijke Friesen

House of Anansi Press is grateful for the privilege to work on and create from the Traditional Territory of many Nations, including the Anishinabeg, the Wendat, and the Haudenosaunee, as well as the Treaty Lands of the Mississaugas of the Credit.

 Canada Council   Conseil des Arts   ONTARIO ARTS COUNCIL
for the Arts   du Canada   CONSEIL DES ARTS DE L'ONTARIO
an Ontario government agency
un organisme du gouvernement de l'Ontario

With the participation of the Government of Canada | Canadä
Avec la participation du gouvernement du Canada

We acknowledge for their financial support of our publishing program the Canada Council for the Arts, the Ontario Arts Council, and the Government of Canada.

Printed and bound in Canada

For my parents

For my parents

We scattered quickly like sheep—
We gathered, weak—
We became morsels in the stomach of a whale.
—AHMAD S. TEEBI (translated from the Arabic)

CONTENTS

CONTENTS

HER FIRST PALESTINIAN

Not long after the first joys of finding each other had settled, Nadia asked me if I would teach her about my country. It was inevitable. The walls of my Toronto apartment were conspicuously covered with Palestinian artifacts, and donation brochures featuring Gazan children were often lying around.

I said of course I would, though at the time I was busy finishing up my residency and trying to land a permanent position. She was busy too; she was a lawyer.

Our initial discussions were informal and took place between embraces. After she quickly devoured the basics and asked for more, I realized I had to create a sort of ad hoc curriculum for Nadia. So I did. I summarized all the major historical milestones (the British Mandate, the Nakba, the 1967 war, et cetera), and supplemented with analyses of

1

current socio-political issues. Most of these things I knew by heart, like any good diasporic offspring. For those that I didn't, I asked my parents, or consulted a text I trusted. I took an even-handed approach, because someone as intelligent as Nadia would've been wary of anything less.

I am no proselytizer, but the truth was self-evident. Nadia took to the cause immediately. She had a lot of outrage.

"Do you realize that you are an indigenous population?" she asked. I did.

"Do you realize that they are trying to prevent you from engaging in even the most peaceful forms of protest?" she demanded. I did.

I attributed most of Nadia's reaction to her desire to support me. But some of it seemed to stem from her feeling that she had been duped: that all her life, she had been taught one thing, when the reality I was revealing to her was something far different.

About a month into our relationship, after a morning of drinking mint tea and discussing the Second Intifada, Nadia appeared to get fed up. She rose from her seat and pushed me roughly onto the floor. Before I could stagger back up, she pushed me again. Not knowing what to do, I laughed. But she wanted to fight. I was uncomfortable with wrestling a woman, but Nadia's jabs were persuasive. I began to wrestle back, only defensively, making sure not to exert too much pressure. Nadia did her best to pummel me. She pressed herself into my flesh and tried to immobilize me under her grip. The floors of my studio apartment were bare. My skin smouldered in pain as she jerked my body back and forth against the parquet.

Later, she apologized for her outburst. "I'm sorry. I just find that these days I am filled with a fighting energy that I need to release," she said. "But I shouldn't have acted that way."

"Forget it," I said. "It's okay."

Over the next few weeks, I sent Nadia articles that I thought would interest her: a news story about another incident at a checkpoint, or a breakdown of the peace plan of the day. She sent back massive polemics, decrying the actions of the occupying military, wondering how a child so young could end up eyeless or armless from the volleys of grown soldiers. My inbox filled with Nadia's responses. Whenever I next saw her, she would expand on her points, and add more that she had thought of in the intervening time. I could not have been prouder. I felt like someone, unexpectedly, had understood a hidden part of me.

One time, I showed Nadia a passport that belonged to my grandfather, which I had long treasured and kept out of sight. It was leather-brown, torn, and dated 1945. Nadia held it with care and protection. The covers said

"Palestine" in three languages, including Hebrew. "That's important," Nadia pointed out. She posted a picture of it online, captioned "Evidence."

"Thank you for doing that," I said. "Every little bit helps."

Nadia did not reply. Instead, she tensed her body into a ready position. She whistled, then lunged at me. My chest crumpled where she struck me with the top of her head. As I lay on my back, she ground her knee into my stomach and asked if I wanted to give up.

"Get off," I said.

She stood up, leaving me in a heap on the floor. "I thought you would struggle harder than you did," she said.

More and more, it was Nadia who sent me the articles. She uncovered new independent media outlets that I did not know, more honest reporters, less fearful opinion writers. I responded to her forwards at first but eventually gave up and left them mostly unread. My inbox had simply grown too full.

In spring, I was granted an interview for a radiology position at Sunnybrook Hospital, my first choice. Nadia had just been promoted to partner, the youngest at her firm. But she hardly had time to celebrate, as she was in the midst of litigating a major investor fraud case. We were a team, supporting one another in our battles: Nadia peppering me with interview questions and helping me refine my answers, and me listening to her rehearse her oral argument and trying to find holes in it.

At bedtime, when we were both usually exhausted, she made a habit of asking me to read her some Mahmoud Darwish, in the original Arabic, even though she could not understand it. She wanted to drift away to his words as I spoke them.

Once, she woke up feverish, in a sweat. "Abed!" she cried, still in the delirium of sleep. "I had a horrible dream that we were running out of time and Palestine was almost gone. We need more help. Should we be starting to have children?"

As a policy, I did not introduce any women to my family. There was no need to trouble them with anyone until I was ready to marry. So it was no small matter when I asked my parents if I could bring someone called Nadia (not an Arab, I clarified) to meet them. My father was dismayed because, as a soon-to-be doctor, my stock was quite high in the community, and there were choices. My mother was too sad to say anything.

While Nadia and I were on a midsummer hike near some waterfalls, I got an email on my phone from Sunnybrook offering me the position. Nadia jumped and clapped at the news. Later, as we navigated a tricky hill, she asked if I knew of any Palestinian lawyers. She wanted to use her expertise to get involved in the cause in a more serious way. I referred her to my friend Salwa, who ran an activist legal group in the city.

When we got home, Nadia called Salwa, introduced herself, and they talked for over an hour. They ended by setting up a coffee date. Putting her phone down, Nadia ran to where I was seated on the sofa, flew hip-first into my stomach, then gripped me in a furious headlock. She squeezed my neck in the crook of her elbow until I was out of breath and choking against her chest. Instinctively, I threw her off, and she clattered to the floor, cackling with excitement at my aggression.

I was upset at her, and also at myself, for reacting in such an uncontrolled way. Before she could come at me again, I stood up and said, "Nadia, we need to talk about this thing you do. Do you actually want me to fight back, or not? I don't want to hurt you." But Nadia was not interested in such a discussion. She said talking would only fetishize it. This was not a fetish, she said, it was important.

Within half an hour of her arrival at my parents' house to meet them for the first time, Nadia had changed their minds. She knew all about the small town in Palestine where they came from and recounted to them all the heroes of that town's resistance.

"What a woman," my father whispered to me in the kitchen as he tasted some fried pine nuts. "*Smart* woman, *strong* woman," he continued. My mother allowed herself a slight smile as she spooned rice into a serving dish.

The next day, Nadia's trial concluded. Her managing partner took the opportunity to call her into his office and inform her that some of the firm's large corporate clients had complained about Nadia's strident social media posts.

"I told him I didn't give a shit," said Nadia. "Anyway, I took some time off, since the trial is over." Apparently, Salwa was scheduled to visit the West Bank to work with a local legal aid agency, and she had invited Nadia to tag along. Nadia had excitedly accepted.

Around that time, I went to a home decor store and purchased an inexpensive area rug, to soften the burden on our grappling bodies.

I HAD BEEN at my new job for a little over a month, and already I was quite well regarded. My father had told me, "Represent us with kindness," and I tried my best to do so. The nurses loved working with this new Dr. Abed, and my fellow doctors respected him. Meanwhile, I told every sympathetic ear I knew that my partner, Nadia (not even an Arab, I clarified), was spending her precious vacation time on a trip to the West Bank, doing everything in her power to help.

Nadia's industriousness was awe-inspiring. Despite being unable to formally take on clients because she was not licensed there, she involved herself in cases anyway. Over Nadia's three weeks in the West Bank (Salwa had come back home after just one), our phone calls became a daily accounting of the sheer variety of human suffering, intermingled with shreds of "I love you," and "I miss you," and "I want to be in your arms." Her social media posts were even more detailed: one day it was the story of a fifth member of the same family thrown into prison without charges; another day it was a journalist brutalized for turning her camera towards a protest. It seemed that every time we spoke, Nadia and her team were about to head to court to argue for interim release, or for an appeal from an unjust sentence, or for simple access to detained clients, or something.

I tried to turn our conversations to lighter topics. On a video call, I showed her my biceps and joked that I had been going to the gym more often, training to defeat her. Nadia let out a hollow laugh. She told me about another man she was representing, this one accused of rolling a flaming car tire into a passel of soldiers who had been guarding the teardown of his family's home.

In her whole stay, I don't think Nadia even took the time to smell the air of the Dead Sea.

When she came back, Nadia slept for an entire day at my place. Her skin, roasted by the region, had gone from fair to olive. The following day was a Monday. We dressed together, for the first time both as professionals, and walked to the subway, taking opposite trains to work.

After dinner that evening, Nadia was walking to the bathroom when I brushed her shoulder, purposely, a twinkle of mischief in my eye. She did not notice.

In bed, she held my hand in hers. "I forgot how soft your hand is," she said. Then she twisted it, but gently, and fell asleep.

Nadia was assigned several new cases at her firm, but she settled them all in short order, within weeks. She frequently took afternoons off to come home, where she would turn on her computer and draft court documents for the one Palestinian client she kept, the tire roller, Kamal. Over the phone, she argued about strategy with her West Bank co-counsel, occupying them late into the night in their time zones. In the mornings, if I woke up early enough, I might catch her in the sunny alcove of my living room, discussing the particulars of Kamal's case with him, and asking after his parents and siblings.

Nadia's partners at the firm noticed her waning commitment. "I've been given a warning," she told me one day. She had frequently been heard discussing Kamal's case on her phone at work, and found high-profile opportunities to speak about Palestinian rights in the media. I had not known of any of these appearances or articles, so I was surprised. The partners told her to either tone it down or risk losing her job. "But let's be real," she said. "I'm a full partner and the best lawyer in that firm. Let's see them try and take me down."

I counselled her to be more circumspect, if she could. By now, thanks to Nadia, the cause had become a constant concern in my life. In her presence, it became difficult to live normally, or to talk about anything else.

Nadia's wrestling came back with her, but it was different. Now, she rarely took me by surprise. Instead, she asked: "Do you want to get on the floor?" When I did, her movements were listless, mechanical. It seemed she was doing it mostly for my sake, to keep alive some tradition we had.

My parents were growing impatient with me. Even my mother asked: "When will you marry her, Abed? We saw her on the news the other day, talking about us, *about us*. She has raised our heads so high, *so high!*"

I was comfortably liquid from my new position and flush with credit from expectant banks. I started looking for a house to replace my tiny apartment.

For our first anniversary, I took Nadia to a restaurant to celebrate. She wore a shimmering green dress with a red rose in her dark hair. She looked content.

As our appetizer was being cleared, she received a notification on her phone and almost leapt out of her seat with joy. She showed me why: it was a feature article, published in the *Globe*, about the controversial Middle East case being handled by an enterprising young Canadian lawyer.

"This will get so much publicity for Kamal's case," she sighed, the corners of her eyes welling. The story included a picture foregrounding Kamal, an angular-faced, dark-complexioned fellow, with Nadia and her Jerusalem co-counsel looming behind him, arms crossed. The story portrayed Kamal, "a humble seller of snacks and sundries from East Jerusalem," in a surprisingly sympathetic light.

That weekend, I browsed in stores for plush Oriental carpets to outfit my prospective new house. Obligingly, Nadia came with me. She smiled and shook her head at my exchanges with the store clerks.

"What's the matter?" I asked.

She said that listening to me brought back memories of Kamal's family, who had to hurry to collect their carpets as they were kicked out of their house. They needed those carpets so that they would have something to lay on the dirt when they, newly homeless, slept outside.

On Sunday night, Nadia held me by my soft hands on the sofa and asked if I thought it would be okay for her to take a temporary leave of absence from her work so that she could go assist with Kamal's preliminary hearings. She explained that she had no long-term cases on the go, and her partners would probably enjoy a respite from dealing with lobbying groups sending complaint letters about her activities. It would be maybe three months of work, but so critical to the case.

"Abed, I understand you probably can't take so much time off so early in your career," she said. "But maybe you could come for vacation for a week or so while I'm there?"

My hands were still nestled in Nadia's, but she was gazing past me.

"Are you in love with him?" I replied.

Nadia did not lunge at me. She did not move a muscle.

I said to myself, just let her, let her go to him, let her go, let her go to her first Palestinian.

DO NOT WRITE ABOUT THE KING

By now I've had a chance to reflect on my father's advice over the years that I knew him, and I've come to the conclusion that the great bulk of it was sound and wise. The great bulk of it, also, I rejected with great prejudice. As I always told him, there's more than one way to live a life.

My father took to the argeeleh again in his last days. He would sit in our back garden in suburban Toronto, with a hose dangling from one side of his mouth, the other side releasing artfully measured puffs of green apple–flavoured smoke, perfuming the limbs of our old black willow above him. The grand sultan of the corner of Mavis and Burnhamthorpe, him. He had a fatalistic view of his skin cancer, now relapsed, so he could no longer be talked out of enjoying a late-afternoon smoke every day, or a few squares of my mother's nammoura when she made it. By then — this was in 2019 — he'd had so many of those sweet semolina cakes that there was hardly any breathing room left in his drawstring pyjama pants, their accordion waist stretching taut around his enlarged belly. Well, maybe it was half the nammoura, half the prednisone.

My father was on his usual back garden roost for an after-dinner tea on a mild Sunday in August. With one foot tucked under the opposite thigh, he batted away the late-summer flies with his free copy of *Arab Toronto News*. The whole of our small family was gathered around him: my mother; my older sister, Amani; and me. Amani and my mother chattered among themselves; it had recently been leaked to Amani that she would be receiving an endowed Chair in economics at the university, and my mother was making a fuss over it for her. I nudged the charcoals around on the argeeleh tray and tried to interest my father in news of the local soccer team. One of the neighbourhood's feral rabbits made fleeting appearances around the marigold bushes, and we couldn't help but smile at it, except for my mother, who was worried about the marigolds. The tan-bricked house, the only family home we knew in Canada, hulked behind us affably.

"I've seen the latest piece you wrote in your column," my father said to me. He finished slurping the shrubby dregs of his tea. "And I want you to take it down."

This command quieted the women's conversation.

It took a moment before I understood what he meant. I did not have a "column," but, as an assistant professor of mathematics at the university, I had to maintain a professional website with a running list of my publications and research interests. It also included a blog, which I updated so rarely that I generally forgot it existed. But two days ago I had added an entry headlined "Clear Your Weekend Schedule: New Article by Yours Truly in *Geometry and Topology*, Now Online."

"I didn't know you read my site, baba." I feigned surprise, but mostly I was annoyed that his watchful eye had extended even to my pointless blog.

"I have always been interested in what you do, Murad."

A model of patience, I inquired: "And what exactly needs to be taken down?" I looked at my mother and then Amani, who both seemed worried that one of our familiar confrontations was to come.

"You made some remarks about the King of _____. You can't do that, Murad. Do not write about the King."

I had made one remark, yes. For my blog, I'd extracted from my paper a model made up of scattershot points on a graph. After summarizing its mathematical interest, I had, in a flippant moment, added:

Interestingly, this same graph is used by the King of _____ to determine hiding spots for the body parts of his critics.

❧

AMANI AND I often disagreed on the best way to deal with our father. She felt that, in his old age, it was kindest to just give him what he wanted, to make him happy. Wasn't this why, earlier this year, we had left our comfortable condos in the city and come back to live with him and our mother in our old home? Why not complete his contentment? Let him sail into that darkness as himself, our beloved protector and patriarch, with us as his doting, obedient children.

"He only has so many months left, Murad. Why make them difficult?" Amani said.

I felt that treating a dying man like an infant would insult and hurt him. My father was still alert, and still involved in our lives. Nearly every weekend, our entire extended family in Canada congregated at his house, and he received them all. He remembered all their children's favourite toys and foods, the plot lines of their work lives, their angsts and histories. He involved himself with them at the minutest levels, recalling stories about their parents, correcting everything from postures to viewpoints, and imploring that more Arabic be spoken. He had done this for the thirty-some years that we had lived here, and he still did.

I told Amani that our father deserved to be treated with vigour because, within that sickly body, his mind still churned as it always had. Acquiescing so easily to him would be like letting this old boxer train with dummies.

"AND, JUST SO I'm clear, why can't I write about the King?"

"What is the use of what you wrote? And yet think of the possible harm."

"What harm are you talking about?"

"Don't you know what the King does?"

"I know very well what he does, thank you. But there are many, many others who speak and write about how horrible he and his Kingdom are. It's not just me."

"Just because there are many like you doesn't mean *you* will escape their attention."

"We're ten thousand kilometres away from the Kingdom, baba."

"And you think they don't have ten thousand ways to assert themselves on us?"

"Never mind that we're talking about my obscure little blog, which is visited by me and you and probably no other soul."

"It has your name and our family name on it, where you live and work."

"So what?"

"Murad, wouldn't you like to visit the Kingdom sometime?"

"Never."

"Okay ... Wouldn't you like your family to have the option to visit the Kingdom?"

"Couldn't care less if they ever do. Prefer that they don't."

"Wouldn't you at least like your relatives in the Kingdom, or those in the orbit of the Kingdom, to live in peace?"

WHEN I WAS a child we lived in the Kingdom, though we were never its subjects. It was always clear that we were just visitors, a few more Palestinians blown there like specks of a sandstorm, and our hosts seemed in perpetual wait for us to be blown away again. We treated their sick, built their villas and commercial complexes, and taught their children, but why should that matter? Every six months my parents were made to appear at an acrid-aired government office to obtain confirmation that we may continue to enjoy the privileges of existing in the Kingdom. My father, in a long queue of foreigner fathers like him, would have his eyes downcast, his residency renewal forms clutched with both hands over the front of his trousers, and his broad shoulders curved inwardly to diminish himself, as he waited for the surly post-teen in a uniform to nod him over for processing. *I promise that I won't trouble the Kingdom much*, his comportment seemed to say.

Relatively speaking, we had it easy. My father rose to the post of lead engineer on the construction projects of several large medical facilities in the capital city, projects commissioned by the Kingdom's moneyed government. Day after day, he ventured into the vast sepias of that desert, letting its heat spider into his flesh as he directed workers to create marvels that the Kingdom's best and brightest could not. The law of the Kingdom did not permit him to own the company he founded (only a Kingdomite could), nor could he be its chief executive, but he had the good fortune of befriending a trustworthy citizen who agreed to take only half of the company's profits in exchange for signing his name on its registration papers. My mother, for her part, was the only woman mathematics professor in the capital's university, an honour she made sure to keep from her acquaintances—you never knew which senior bureaucrat or other was in search of a good position to pluck away for his freshly graduated son.

I did well, too, excelling in all my subjects at the English school my parents enrolled me in, though I was prouder of my encyclopedic command of the expurgated plot lines of *Knight Rider* and *Perfect Strangers*. Often I imagined myself deriding my classmates to their faces in an English far above their level of understanding—the confidence they derived from actually having a country would be no match for my intimidating TV education. Unfortunately, my father enforced a strict policy of polite deference to Kingdomites. So instead, I contented myself with performing cartoonish imitations of them to my sister in our bedrooms. I kept Amani laughing for hours.

"Habeebi, if I wanted to, I could have your father, and your father's father, kicked out of our nation by tomorrow, and all the kisses you rain down on my feet could not get them back," I would bluster, spoiling my Arabic with their dialect's snorts and fricatives, their pompousness dripping from my every word.

Once, our cackles got too loud to escape notice, and my father stormed into the room and shut my show down. "It would be nice if you could learn to be grateful for what the Kingdom has given us," he said, "and careful not to squander it."

My father himself was so overcome with gratitude that not a month went by that he did not bring home a fresh immigration application, crinkled and dog-eared but aglow with promise. So many countries grinned in our supposed future. America, of course, was the first choice (at least back in those days), but there was also Canada, Australia, the U.K., Germany (though we'd have to learn German), or maybe even a wild card like Chile or Argentina. My parents never discussed their plans with us children.

"They want us to think there's nothing wrong with where we live now," my sister said, rolling her eyes.

We loved listening to the adults indulge in their escape fantasies. Even back in those days, our house—my father's house—was the weekly destination for all of our relatives and close friends. My mother's cooking had much to do with it, but there was something about my father's caring for everyone, and his success in the Kingdom, that made everyone want to draw closer to him, and listen to him.

Late in the evenings of those gatherings, when the hubbub of all the food and the drink had receded, that's when the best secrets of our Kingdom-free future could be overheard, if your ears were sharp enough. My father would get up from his customary spot on the veranda, pick up the floppy-armed argeeleh, and bring it, together with an uncle or two, inside with him. Lowering their voices and thinking they were out of earshot of the children, they would debate the merits of each destination. Australia had its weather, Canada had its friendly people, Argentina had Maradona. Each family member had a preference, and each voiced it like they were savouring a taste in their mouths.

My father's perspective was more grounded. "Let's not kid ourselves," I once heard him say to one of my uncles. "We won't really get to choose. Wherever we get accepted first, that will be our first and best choice."

Until that time, my father toiled under the Kingdom's sun, which broiled its cancer into him every day.

🌢

"I'M NOT GOING to take it down," I told my father.

"So I suppose that you learned nothing from what happened to your cousin Omar?" he answered.

"I learned never to set foot in the Kingdom. But I'm not willing to learn any more."

My father opened his mouth to speak again, but something caught in his throat. He fell into a fit of violent coughing that left his eyes red, his chest undulating like a disturbed pool. Amani rushed to pat his back. My mother ran to the kitchen to get him a cup of water.

"Enough!" Amani said, glaring at me. And then, to my father: "Baba, why do you concern yourself with his dumb little jokes? Let him have them; he's like a child."

MY COUSIN OMAR is an unobtrusive accountant, harmless as a smudge. He lives in Mississauga, too, like us. Last year, he took his wife, Nuha, and his two daughters on a vacation to Hong Kong. Their way back home included a stopover in the Kingdom. At the gate, Nuha and the children were permitted to board the plane back to Toronto, but Omar was told that there were some issues with his paperwork, and he would have to wait a few hours until the next flight.

But a whole day after Nuha had arrived home, she had not heard from Omar. She tried calling his cellphone many times, to no avail—it went directly to voice mail. She also wasn't able to reach anyone at the airport who knew what had become of him.

On the second day, she came to see my father, who had kept an eye on Omar ever since Omar's own father died a few years back. Alarmed at hearing what happened, my father took over the long-distance search for his nephew. He still had some contacts at the Kingdom's Ministry of Public Works; during his years in Canada, he had carefully maintained good relations with them by providing professional consultations, both formal and informal, whenever he was asked. And so my father now made dozens of calls, addressing the men on the other side of the phone with every honorific he could think of, his mouth permanently stretched into a sickening rictus of ingratiation. He also tried to marshal the help of some friends who had remained in the Kingdom, and who knew other officials in other ministries. He did this for hours every day. Most of the time, he was met with sympathetic words and promises to see what could be done. Nothing of real use.

Trying to be helpful, I suggested flexing some muscle by contacting the Canadian embassy and the press. I even volunteered the name of a friend who worked in a law firm that dealt in similar international situations.

My father waved me off with his hand. "We are trying to get your cousin back safely, not make big statements that will anger people," he said.

Meanwhile, Nuha, unable to stop herself, looked up recent cases of disappearances linked to the Kingdom. A few of them had ended with a grisly death, but most were never resolved, the fate of the disappeared demanded for years by families unable to find closure for their grief. Nuha kept reading the stories, imagining the worst outcomes, and bursting into tears.

On the fourth day, she finally received a call from her husband.

"They say they will release me soon," Omar said. He would not specify what was happening. "They just have some questions for me."

Five days after that—in total, more than a week after his family had been back—Omar called from Pearson Airport: "Please come get me," he told Nuha.

We visited his house the following morning. He looked tired, and his voice was faint. He evaded our questions, pulling nervously on the short hairs of his beard.

"It's better that he doesn't tell us any more anyway," my father said. "Let's be thankful he made it out safely and stop pestering him with questions."

Unsatisfied, I prodded Omar some more, but all he disclosed was that, as far as he could tell, there was someone with the same name and background that the Kingdom wanted to arrest. They assumed *our* Omar was that person, and the officers who handled him were going to ask him questions until they could prove that he was. They persisted like this for days. During the time that Omar wasn't being questioned, he was left alone in a fluorescent-lit cell, with only a bench seat and a metal toilet.

Eventually someone, somewhere, determined that Omar was not the person the Kingdom was after. They let him go.

We never found out if my father's interventions had anything to do with it.

A FEW DAYS after our disagreement about my blog, I knew I had to be the one to make up with my father, since I had clearly instigated the matter by holding a view that differed from his.

I called him from my university office. His voice on the phone was tired and almost inaudible. It seemed like he was having one of his bad days, when his body was seared by pain and his resolve lowered. I tried to cheer him up by talking about one of his pet subjects, my and Amani's careers. I told him that my paper in *Geometry and Topology* had become a minor sensation in my field. It elicited three letters to the editor that were published on the journal's online site, one of which proposed an interesting (if misguided) logarithmic correction to one of my terms. My time at the office these days was often interrupted by fellow professors and researchers calling to discuss my paper and suggest possible collaborations in the future.

Amani's career was flourishing, too, I told him, even more than mine. Her office was two floors up, and most times when I popped in, she was busy completing a biographical questionnaire or an end-of-year report, in preparation for her announcement as the new Chair in International Economics and Finance. I even saw her on the campus steps posing for professional photos to accompany an upcoming article on her in the alumni journal. The thought of his first-born daughter being feted in this way lifted my father's spirits some.

Finally, I asked: "Are you still upset with me?"

My father sighed, and seemed to weigh his words. "It was never a matter of being upset. I just want what is best for you and the family."

"I know that," I said.

"And I like to think I know some small things about how to make sure you live a happy and safe life."

"Baba, I won't take it down."

My father was silent for a moment. Then, because he could not resist, he reached for one of his classic tactics: highlighting his weakness in the hope that I would feel sorry for him and relent. "I can hardly force you to do anything, my son. I'm just an old man now," he said, "close to my time."

"Your time is still very, very far off, inshallah," I said. I was not going to change my mind. No matter how hard my father was trying to force his fear on me, that was an inheritance in which I wanted no part.

I EXPECTED THAT the matter was closed. I expected that I would be vindicated, that neither my father nor I would ever have cause to think about any of that Kingdom nonsense again. In a way, it still shocks me that this is not what happened.

The first thing that did happen was that my cousin Omar had to go to the Kingdom. The accounting firm where he worked was conducting an audit on a company headquartered in the capital city, and the client required that he attend on-site for two weeks.

Nuha was exceptionally agitated by this news. In no uncertain terms, she forbade Omar from leaving. Instead of listening to her, he booked his tickets and his hotel. Nuha escalated her campaign by calling on the rest of the family, first among them my father, to try to dissuade him. Phone calls shot back and forth between various family members, expressing opinions and worries.

Reprising his usual role, my father invited everyone to our house to talk it over. It was one of the last warm days of fall. The sun was dignified and affectionate, the remaining foliage on our black willow the colour of dark raspberries. But this was a matter for inside.

Everyone stuffed into our living room: two aunts with their husbands, four cousins with their spouses, and a gaggle of children. We planned to eat dinner first and talk after, but no sooner had we picked up our plates and begun filling them than the beseeching started.

"We almost lost our minds last time. Does that not matter to you?" said Nuha, chorused by the rest of the family. "So what if you lost a damn promotion, or even your whole job?"

"Who walks into the belly of a beast like this?" yelled Omar's brother, his fork stabbing the air in Omar's direction.

"It ended well the last time, but why tempt fate?" lamented Omar's mother, rubbing her hands together in distress.

My father asked everyone to calm down and understand that Omar's point of view was valid as well, that his work was important, after all. But—and this he directed to Omar—perhaps there was a way to do the work from here, without venturing to the Kingdom? Perhaps a family emergency could be invented as an excuse?

"Because when it comes to the Kingdom, I prefer to avoid even the smallest of risks," he said, and brought up his advice to me about my blog as an example. The reproachful eyes of my mother and aunts flitted momentarily from Omar to me.

"I have no choice in the matter, ammi," Omar said, diffidently. "I am so close to becoming partner. I can't just say I won't go. It's not reasonable. This time, I am going as part of a team, for business. And anyway, I have faith that it has all been straightened out with the Kingdom since last time."

I chimed in: "I'm with Omar. Nothing out of the ordinary will happen. Omar will go, and he will come back, on time and safe."

And so, Omar boarded a plane, spent twenty hours in transit, and called Nuha from his layover in Frankfurt. He texted her when the wheels hit the hot asphalt of the Kingdom.

After that, she did not hear from him.

Give him a moment to catch his breath down there, she was told. *No doubt you will laugh and laugh at these tears of yours when that rascal finally pipes up*, she tried to tell herself.

After two days, Nuha contacted her husband's firm. They, too, had not heard from Omar, and in fact had already replaced him on the project (with someone working remotely, they mentioned, to Nuha's outrage).

My father began dialing long-distance numbers again. The same contacts in the Ministry of Public Works, the same friends who knew officials in other ministries. This time, my father slathered a topping of apology on top of the nauseating servility that accompanied his requests.

"I offer my eternal gratitude, and that of my wife, my daughter, and my son, if you could forgive our intrusion and favour us by asking—just a few small words of inquiry—after my nephew Omar, who I'm certain is the victim of a totally understandable misunderstanding that is not at all the fault of the Kingdom, but my nephew's alone." It got so bad I took to immediately exiting any room in which he raised a phone to his ear.

This time, most of those he contacted were less sympathetic.

"From your repeated inquiries, it seems there is a real problem with this nephew you are asking after, Abu-Murad," one of his friends at the Ministry told him. "If he keeps getting in trouble with the Kingdom, no doubt there is a reason. Our Kingdom is not composed of buffoons, or—no matter what your Western press says—monsters."

My father asked Nuha, "Do you know if Omar has done anything the Kingdom would not condone? He never seemed rash in that way to me."

By this time, my father was quite frail. His body was reacting poorly to the latest round of chemotherapy. He had grown exceptionally large, and his entire mass shuddered even as he sat doing nothing. He could no longer hold the hose of his argeeleh without someone (usually my sister) steadying it for him. He stopped to catch his breath in the middle of most sentences, so listening to him became an exercise in patience in even more ways. But none of this deterred him from making inquiries about Omar, trying to pull at every last strand of pity in the hearts of those faceless men in the faraway Kingdom, the men who seemed so uninvested in my father and his nephew, so unmotivated to lift even a finger to help us.

Over and over, my father would take a deep breath, ready his saccharine words, and dial.

"AMANI, DO YOU remember the day before we left the Kingdom to come to Canada?"

"Very well."

"You were how old, twelve? I was seven, I think."

"Thirteen and eight, actually."

"Baba took us to his work with him, to help carry out his things."

"You insisted on carrying all the boxes, one after the other, to the car, trying to be a big man."

"Do you remember what his boss said when he saw us?"

"It wasn't his boss, exactly. It was the deputy minister," she reminded me.

Before our father's last day at work, we had never met the deputy minister of Public Works, though we felt we knew him. On many occasions we had overheard our father drop his name triumphantly into the after-work stories with which he regaled our mother.

— "The deputy minister came to the work site today and was completely shocked at the progress we had made. You should have seen how his eyes lit up!"

— "The deputy minister specifically asked for me, by name. He said I was — and I quote — 'a shining star in the Kingdom's constellation of engineers'!"

— "My goodness, habeebti! The deputy minister said he might invite us to his house for the second day of Eid!"

This deputy minister seemed to us the most exceptional Kingdomite, our father's greatest and most privileged ally. Someone who actually understood our worth.

The deputy minister I saw on our last day did not match what I had envisioned. He was a thin stalk of a man, with matte, apathetic eyes. He looked at my father and me, holding boxes outside my father's office, and shook his head, as if he had caught us stealing. My father began his usual words of deference, but the deputy minister waved him to silence.

The deputy minister said he was surprised that he had to hear of my father's imminent departure second-hand, from one of his subordinates, and not from my father himself. He said he was surprised that whichever employer in Canada was so eager to hire my father had not given his prime benefactor in the Kingdom a call. He thought they were keen on references and such in Canada, or was that not the case? The deputy minister said that if he had received such a call, he would've informed that rash Canadian employer that although my father showed some promise at his job, it was the Kingdom's grace that enabled him to accomplish so much. It was the Kingdom that gave my father those glamorous, high-profile projects that no doubt sparkled in his resumé. It was the Kingdom that forgave my father's mistakes in design and execution, and allowed him to spend money to correct them. It was the Kingdom that paid my father enough that his savings looked attractive to Canada and who knows what other opportunistic countries he had applied to. It was the Kingdom that authorized its reporters to interview my father and put his name in stories covering all those grand openings. It was the Kingdom that, in the first place, gave my father a home and security, after his whole family was scattered and unwanted. And who knows? said the deputy minister. If my father had continued to progress under its auspices, the Kingdom might have, after a long and happy career, bestowed on my father its top awards and honours for his life's work. My father could have been a legend and an exemplar to Kingdomites and non-Kingdomites alike.

But all that is gone now, said the deputy minister. The decisions people make are baffling, are they not?

My father looked at the ground in silence during this speech. Finally, he began to reply that he hoped the Kingdom would forgive him because he had always loved and respected the King, the Kingdom, and its citizens — but the deputy minister had already walked away without waiting for him to finish.

IN LATE NOVEMBER, a month after Omar had disappeared, Nuha finally received a call from him. She hurried over to our house with the news. I sat on a chair, tending to my father as he lay on the sofa, his upper back propped against a pillow. He had spent most of the day curled in pain but straightened himself to hear Nuha.

"I can hardly believe it, ammi. Omar said that it was the *same exact* problem as last time. They think he is someone else, a higher-up in some organization that they banned."

My father winced, seemingly doubly pained.

"How is this happening again?" Nuha asked.

"Is he being mistreated?" managed my father.

"He didn't say. You know Omar. But I'm so worried. He said they plan to hold him until they're absolutely sure this time. And who knows when that will be?"

I said, "Do they actually think that someone they banned would simply traipse into the Kingdom on a commercial flight, with a regular passport that has his actual name on it, like it's nothing? This is utter insanity."

"Omar mentioned something else," said Nuha. "He said they asked about you, ammi, and you, Murad."

I was thunderstruck. "Excuse me?"

"They asked about you by name."

I tried to collect my thoughts, without success. "What... what did they ask about?"

"If Omar knew you."

"And? Anything else?"

"How would I know? We didn't get a chance to talk about anything else. My whole call with him was exactly three minutes. That was all the time he was allowed."

My father tried to speak, but his lips only quivered weakly before he surrendered and let them rest again. Instead, he moved the muscles of his brow enough to look at me from the corner of his eye. Then he closed both eyes and swallowed with difficulty.

Even in his frailty he knew how to accuse me.

"This situation is getting more and more absurd," I said.

Later that night, when Nuha had left and I was alone in my room, I went to my blog. I had not updated it since my disagreement with my father. There were still no comments on my last post, the one that besmirched the King's reputation. I looked at the traffic counter. Precious few had even seen the blog, a total of fourteen unique visits in two months. Nine of those were from within my university, two from elsewhere in Toronto, and one each from New York and the Netherlands, where two of my collaborators lived.

One visit, however, was from an address that mapped to the Kingdom.

"SO YOU WILL take it down then, right?"

"Amani, please, not you, too."

"But your idiotic little joke has now gotten you on the lists of those goons who have Omar!"

"Maybe so, or maybe it was just some Bedouin interested in new advances in differential geometry. We don't actually know anything."

"What is the matter with you? Our father is almost dead, and you're trying to prove some kind of point? Why are you like this, Murad?"

I didn't know why I was like this.

AROUND CHRISTMASTIME, our yard was blanketed with snow and stillness. My father was pharmaceutically asleep most of the time, and unable to make any more phone calls when he was awake. Anyway, he had run out of people to call and favours to ask. When he was alert, he spent his hours staring at pundits arguing on the news programs of Middle East satellite stations and being fed spoonfuls of flavourless mush from my mother's hand. His argeeleh stood in a corner of the living room, where it had gone untouched for weeks.

Some time ago I had written to my district represent-ative, demanding action for Omar. Then I tried calling that representative, as well as other parliamentarians and bureaucrats whom I thought might take up the cause, or at least make formal inquiries. All I got out of it was a few letters back indicating that they would "study the situa-tion." I wanted to start a petition page, or contact one of the local TV stations, but felt that it might be best to hold off on making a big scene about it.

Nuha started engaging in conspiracy theories about her husband. "He left so little in his bank accounts, all things considered," she said. "What if he has another wife and family in the Kingdom? There are stories like this, you know. What if he's gone for good?" We tried to comfort her, but it was not a situation with which we had much experience.

At the start of the new year, Amani was informed that she had lost her Chair. Actually, as the representative of the selection committee told her, she never had the Chair to begin with. Whoever leaked the news to her before had done so improperly, and it should never have happened. Yes, the selection committee had at one time thought Amani the best choice for the Chair, but later on, the selection committee thought something else. Apologies for the misunderstanding. But not to worry, Professor Amani, you are still a beacon of our university, and your tenure is intact. You may even take copies of the photos from the alumni journal photo shoot for your personal use, if you like.

"Anyway," said Amani, "at least I got some intel about who the well-heeled funders of the Chair are."

"Who are they?" I asked, like an innocent.

BY MARCH, my father's neck, jowls, ears, and clavicle were covered with melanoma's red-brown lesions, sprawled like continents. His liver had been infested with tumours for some time, and the oxygen readings told the doctors that the metastases had likely encroached on his lungs as well.

He was fitted with a ventilator and put in a hospital bed. In the early pandemic days of 2020, hospital precautions were at a fever pitch. Only one of a short, numbered list of guests was allowed to visit him at any one time, gloved, masked, and surveyed. The rest waited their turn at home, or in the car, distanced from the rest of the world. Each of us in our rotation of three took our shifts in one-hour increments, except for my mother, whose grief fractured her grasp on time. She forgot herself for hours by my father's bed, praying and crying.

"If you don't need to be here..." began many an exhausted nurse reciting to us the directives of the day, and to our credit we were always polite in return, even as we cut them off or ignored them. "The protocol is that you must be twelve feet away from the patient, please," but we came close enough to touch his hand every time the staff looked away.

Amani and I began teaching our university courses online instead of in person, though often we simply cancelled classes, slashing away any tracts of curricula that we could. The outside, though crisp and quiet, felt poisonous, so we rarely ventured there. We lost track of nearly everything that was not my father, and the hospital, and the unknown, masked men and women who circled around him there.

One morning, I was at our family home, readying myself for another shift at my father's bedside. Early spring rains started coming down in heavy, loud sheets. I watched the spectacle through our living room window and noticed a large bundle of mail protruding from our neglected mailbox, getting drenched. I ran outside to fetch it, hand covering my head against the rain, and ran back in. I threw the whole bundle on the floor of our front foyer. It was mostly bank statements and delivery service flyers.

A small envelope caught my eye. The postmark was from the Kingdom, which seemed odd to me, like a vestige of a theoretical place that I was no longer sure existed.

It occurred to me that I had to find a letter opener, as my father would be upset if I rashly tore the envelope open and damaged it. I walked through the house for what seemed like an hour looking for one. I looked in nonsensical places, like in my mother's yarn drawer, or under Amani's bed, or in my own laptop carrying case. Eventually, I found one, in the drawer of my father's desk in his upstairs study. The steel of the blade gleamed, smooth and capable. I sat in my father's chair, catching my breath. I looked at my watch but did not register the time.

I sliced through the envelope. There was a single page, printed on the letterhead of the Ministry of Public Works. The letter, addressed to my father, invited him to the capital city for the Festival of Architecture and Construction, a gala event where he would be celebrated as one of the star builders of the Kingdom and given a lifetime achievement award. The letter mentioned that the award came with a significant prize purse. My father's family, including his lone son, Murad, were invited to accompany him to the Kingdom.

The letter concluded: *The Kingdom is your first home, and it would delight and honour the Kingdom if you would permit her to reward you on her loving soil.*

CYNTHIA

For some time in his early twenties, when he was still on his student visa, Nader maintained a relationship with an imaginary girlfriend. It was a pretence that he kept up to fit in with his roommates, who were seeing their own, quite real, women.

Nader did not know Jeff or Harv when he agreed to live with them. He had found them by answering an ad that he saw in the student centre lounge. They seemed surprised that Nader did not argue with paying an equal portion of the rent on their shared house, even though the room they offered him was actually only a tiny den, without so much as a door to close. Nader was just grateful to be taken in. Since he'd arrived in Toronto from his home in Amman a year earlier, he had hardly interacted with anyone, apart from some brief conversations with professors and course administrators. He looked forward to the opportunity to make friends.

The house that Nader moved into was an old semi-detached in the Annex neighbourhood, close to the university. It had a vaguely canine smell, the floors squealed and croaked underfoot, and the walls and window ledges were fat with layers of paint from generations of student renters. Instead of being repelled, Nader felt like he was part of a great tradition somehow.

The feeling extended to his roommates. Jeff and Harv seemed to Nader like archetypes of young adult males of Western society, going about the normal business of life. As far as he could tell, this meant desultory attendance of their classes, near-constant possession of a joint (lit or about to be lit) between their fingers, and a woman apiece materializing after dark to noisily spend the night in their respective rooms.

Nader took a particular interest in his roommates' assortment of women, because he had none of his own. In those days, the thought of even speaking to a woman terrified him. He always expected laughter to follow anytime he opened his mouth, even if it was only to order tea at the cafeteria. If he made himself visible to a woman in any way, he was sure his foreignness would betray him somehow, fluttering from under his garments like gas. Nader was also still affected by years of religious upbringing that mandated a circumspect manner around the opposite sex. He had to reconfirm his continued adherence to such concepts when he called his mother back home.

By contrast, Nader's roommates seemed completely unbounded. The house was a major artery for the flow of women: classmates, friends, sex partners, all streamed in for everything from drinks to snacks to naps to private time with his roommates, as if they were voyagers taking a much-needed respite from the long trips to their homes down the street.

Although Harv—and his acoustic guitar—did his part, Jeff was the main reason for this flow. He met scores of women through his sporadic attendance at meetings of the university's International Students' Society (open even to non-internationals), and attracted them, as he boasted, with nothing more than a standing invitation to show them around the city. He was especially keen on women from newly created or aspiring countries (Bosnia, Catalonia, Palau, et cetera), as such backgrounds marked them as particularly "fresh specimens." As a rule, no woman actually lasted in his life—or in the house—for very long.

Nader expected at least a few remarks from his roommates about his obvious singlehood. Jeff did ask once, "When are we going to see you with a girl, our Arabian friend?" though the question seemed mostly intended to fill the time as Jeff waited for the bathroom to free up.

Harv, the kinder of the two, once motioned at Nader, in a way that bordered on camaraderie, to look out the window at an attractive jogger as she ran by the house. But mostly Nader was ignored by his roommates, who had no real use for him apart from the rent he paid.

Because of that, Nader could not understand, even years later, why he, completely unprompted, announced to Jeff and Harv the existence of Cynthia. He did it as casually as he could, because by then he had learned that one must not seem to be very serious about a woman, especially in the early days.

"That actress looks a lot like this girl I'm kind of seeing," he said, as the three of them watched a TV show one Saturday afternoon. The words *this girl I'm kind of seeing* singed Nader's lips with illicit excitement as he uttered them.

Neither Harv nor Jeff seemed particularly moved by this announcement, and this indifference thrilled Nader even more. It meant that they did not consider the existence of a Cynthia to be out of the realm of possibility. It made Nader feel legitimate as a man.

Over the weeks that followed, Nader dropped more references to Cynthia into the scraps of conversation he had with his roommates. Usually he was parroting things he'd heard Jeff and Harv say. "Ugh, don't you hate it when a girl borrows your shirt and just keeps it?" he ventured once, though of course none of his shirts were missing.

In his mind, Nader began to formulate some parameters for Cynthia's appearance and personality, broad outlines of things he admired in a woman: full lips, a small frame, kindness, and the like. But for him, the process of inventing Cynthia was not so much about who Cynthia was, but *that* Cynthia was. Every mention he made of her felt like a new flower being pinned to his chest; it gave him a romantic, knowing quality.

At some point, Jeff's indifference to Cynthia turned into coolness, and later hostility. Nader first began noticing small changes in Jeff's tone: when Nader said that Cynthia was an engineer, Jeff arched an eyebrow and gave a silent sneer; when Nader mentioned Cynthia had blond hair, Jeff grunted, "A blond, even? For you?" Nader was unsure how to interpret these changes at first, though he understood that perhaps he needed to start downplaying Cynthia.

One incident stood out in particular as truly opening the floodgates of Jeff's harassment. He had been in a good mood at the time, having gotten rid of another girl via a short, icy conversation over the phone.

"That was painless enough," he said, satisfied with himself. As he gnashed on an apple, he asked Nader, almost as if the idea had just occurred to him, "Wait, you're Palestinian, right? Are Palestinian girls hot?" A stream of juice slid down Jeff's goatee as he clamped his jaw on another mouthful. "Assuming they are," he added, "can you introduce me to some?"

Nader did not know any Palestinian women in Canada, and had not developed any proprietary sense over them, but he thought he'd imitate something he'd heard Harv say to Jeff in such instances. With a laugh, Nader replied: "If I did, shouldn't I try to protect them from you?"

Jeff was at first taken aback by Nader's temerity but recovered quickly. "Oh, really?" he said. "You know this would be strictly to pass the time between real, worthwhile dates, right?"

Nader wanted to apologize for his comment, but it was too late. Jeff continued, "And do you think it hasn't occurred to us that this girl you claim to be seeing has never actually shown up in the flesh around here? Do you think we're stupid?"

Over the next few weeks, Jeff's attacks became more frequent and systematic. He seemed to listen closely for every mention that Nader made of Cynthia. He prompted Nader for more descriptions of her and interrogated him on any inconsistencies. Flustered, Nader once mixed up Cynthia's invented allergy (polyester) with Jeff's real one (wool), which gave Jeff an opportunity to taunt him by calling her "Synthetic Cynthia."

Harv was sometimes amused by Jeff's conduct; but other times, he seemed eager to pre-empt it, usually by reaching for his guitar and strumming a song over whatever Jeff was saying. When Nader failed to bring Cynthia up for a few days (which he did in an attempt to fade her away), Jeff demanded to know how she was and pressured Nader into telling long stories about his recent times with her. Nader found it increasingly necessary to construct detailed narratives about him and his girlfriend before coming into contact with Jeff.

Most of all, whenever Nader said something that made Cynthia seem too good for him, Jeff immediately pounced. He always wanted Nader to remember that someone as awkward, inexperienced, and foreign as he was could never have a woman like *that*.

Now, Nader wanted to spend as little time as possible in the house. Early in the morning, he would creep downstairs, sneak in a noiseless bite for breakfast, and leave for the day. He would return late at night to flit up to his room like a ghost. It was a difficult way to live, but there were only a few more months left on the lease. Nader hoped he could survive until then.

IN LATE APRIL, on a drizzly Friday, Nader took his usual place between the stacks in the library, safely ensconced in his favourite carrel. He began this day, as had become his habit, with some time devoted to conceiving more of his girlfriend. He would put on his headphones, close his eyes, and visualize him and Cynthia together: chatting, going out, enjoying themselves. When he thought he had enough material, he would type the day's imaginings into his cellphone to help him remember, in case he needed to draw upon those details later. He was determined to avoid any more slip-ups from hastily devised lies.

Today, Nader imagined that he had gone at lunchtime to Cynthia's apartment, where she was busy preparing for her master's defence. Per Nader's most recent revision, Cynthia was no longer an engineer but instead a student of art history, which Nader considered to be a good indicator of a frivolous person.

"She had to switch after failing many engineering courses," Nader had explained to Jeff some days back, rolling his eyes at Cynthia's stupidity. He hoped Jeff would interpret this to mean that she was more likely to tolerate a relationship with Nader.

Nader reminded himself of where Cynthia's apartment was located, off Bloor Street West. The area was too fashionable, and clotted with hipsters, but Nader had committed to it aloud several times before and felt he could not change it without arousing Jeff's suspicion. The subway he took there was relatively empty given the time of day, just a few indigent people taking endless rides to shelter from the rain. Nader was proud to have thought of this detail.

When he arrived at Cynthia's place, she had not changed from her sleepwear, a hole-ridden Run Ramallah T-shirt (formerly Nader's) and lounge shorts. But this image felt far too attractive, so Nader recast it: when he arrived at Cynthia's place, she was wearing a set of pilly pyjamas that were too small for her and highlighted an unflattering droop in her belly; she had sweat stains on her armpits and was holding a balled-up, dingy rag soaked with what smelled like cleaning liquid, which Nader recognized as his old Run Ramallah T-shirt.

This reception hardened Nader to Cynthia. He hugged her in a perfunctory way, without feeling. As he did so, he noticed that the roots of her hair were a nondescript mousy colour. It had only been dyed blond, as it turned out, and she had not bothered to keep it up, now that she had a boyfriend.

It bothered Nader to change Cynthia. In recent days, he had tinkered with a few minor things; he made her a bit taller and more ungainly, her voice higher pitched, her patience for him ever so slightly thinner. The process felt to Nader like tearing with his own hands a favourite tapestry — both difficult and wrong. But he knew it had to be done. Her hair was just another part of the price he felt compelled to pay.

"I'm sorry," Cynthia said, self-consciously bringing her hands to her hair when she saw Nader's eyes on it, "I know it looks horrible. I'm just so strapped for money these days. I can't afford to go to the hairdresser."

Hearing this sad apology, Nader softened towards his girlfriend again. "Not at all. You look as beautiful as ever," he said.

Cynthia had already set a modest table for their lunch. There were some pieces of pita bread, some green olives, and a dish of the zaatar-flecked labneh that Nader had first introduced her to, which had become one of her staple foods. It always pleased Nader to witness Cynthia's adoption of his influences, which she did with a certain openness of spirit that he had not encountered in other imaginary women.

Now, however, he reconsidered how wise it was for her to possess such a trait. Why would Cynthia change her life, or anything about it, for him? He imagined all the things Jeff would say. Nader knew that he should change the meal to something more ordinary, like cheese and crackers, for example, which he had seen his roommates consume many times before. But, as small a change as it was, he could not bring himself to do it. A smear of labneh was already on Cynthia's lips, filmed in oil. Her newly dark and unkempt hair made her look deliciously feral. She gazed at him with real desire.

It was too hard *not* to let her go on like this.

This is where the narrative got away from Nader. In those weeks when he was mostly exiled from his house,

Nader had spent many hours in Cynthia's company. She was no longer just a rough sketch to him. He came to know her well and eagerly anticipated their time together. He knew that Cynthia was an impossible idealization, but something about how she always seemed to fit into him with ease and willingness made him feel a closeness that he did not want to abandon or destroy.

Nader was not deluded that she was part of his real life. He did not—not ever—believe she really existed. But he did not think he was wrong for resorting to her as a coping mechanism.

And so, on this day, allowing himself to enjoy his lunch with Cynthia—the lunch that she had prepared without any of his interferences or revisions—led him down the familiar, comforting paths of their relationship.

They snickered about some of the mannerisms of Nader's professors and Cynthia's supervisors. She allowed him to poke some fun at the large words in her dissertation—how none of the sentences could possibly mean anything, when it came down to it. She asked about the latest song Harv had been playing to show women how sensitive he was. Nader told her it was "Into the Mystic," causing Cynthia to howl with laughter and say, "That's so perfect." She playfully threw olives at him, splashing Nader in the eye with salty juice. When he ran after her in mock vengeance, she scampered over the sofa and nearly tipped over with it, but he caught her mid-fall and they giggled together. They had excellent sex, as usual, with the unexpected bonus that Cynthia permitted Nader to explore areas of her body that she had formerly forbidden. For a while, even the rain stopped. The noontime sun that lolled upon the pair for that brief time in Cynthia's shitty master's candidate's studio was glorious.

Afterwards, as they lay huddled together on the bed, Nader commented on Cynthia's elegant fingers. At this, she reached to retrieve one of her textbooks from a shelf above her bed. Someone, she said, once told her that she had the fingers, long and supple, of a portrait by El Greco, a Greek artist who had mastered the style of Renaissance Spain, his adopted home. Nader ignored the wrinkle of jealousy inside him that made him wonder who in Cynthia's past had paid her this compliment. Instead, as he held in his palm Cynthia's warm hand, he had to agree.

Nader asked Cynthia if she would take him to the Prado, where she first saw El Greco's work while on a trip to Madrid with her parents when she was a teen.

"I wouldn't dream of going again without you," Cynthia said, and nestled her head into his chest.

In this moment of tenderness, Nader confided in Cynthia that Jeff had been very hostile to him recently. This was a major breakthrough for Nader. To this point, he had avoided complaining to her about his roommates.

He did not want her to see him as the vulnerable victim he often was. But now, as they planned a long future together, he felt safe enough to tell her what he had been made to endure.

Cynthia listened with a look of great compassion. She almost teared up at hearing how merciless Jeff was, how unhelpful Harv was. But she was also restrained and respectful. Nader thought it showed her specialness that she never said something as crass as "Can't you just tell them to stop?" or "Stand up to them! What's the worst that could happen?" She didn't even say, "You are strong enough to overcome this. It will pass."

She understood that he might not be strong enough. She understood that his subordination to Jeff might last forever. Cynthia simply let Nader talk himself into stillness as she caressed his arm.

With that, Nader reluctantly exited his time with Cynthia. He took off his headphones. In his cellphone, he typed what she wore, what they had for lunch, the titles of the specific El Greco artworks they discussed, and everything else that transpired. He then readjusted the drawstring of his hoodie, which he had pulled down to use as a stand-in for Cynthia's fingers. He put the illustrated art history textbook back on the library shelf where he'd found it.

Nader couldn't remember if he'd attended the one or two lectures he had that day. He thought that he probably did go to the cafeteria at least once, for lunch, and probably again later, for another bite before it closed. But all that really stood out was his time in the carrel, alone, by the grimy, wet window. The loudness of the rain caused the usual whispers of other students gossiping with their friends in the library stacks to rise to audible levels. Nader tried to listen to them, in case they said anything useful— something that showed him how people conducted their lives and relationships. Little droplets of human drama were all around him, so close he could almost touch them.

Darkness fell. A half hour before the library closed, Nader reviewed the notes on his phone.

Everything he had written seemed preposterous. What had happened was far, far too good. It was as if he had been writing to satisfy his pitiful, childish fantasies, and not to avoid Jeff's wrath. He was disgusted and angry with his lack of discipline. He could only imagine what embarrassment awaited him with his audience at home if he came back with these stories.

He put his headphones back on. He was again with Cynthia in her bed. The sex had been average, actually. Fine, at best. She had a body, right? What more was there to say about that? Re-creating his moment of weakness, he again confided in her how his roommates had been treating him. This time, she did not listen compassionately. This time she grew impatient with him before he even finished.

She seemed surprised, and a little disgusted, that he had let his roommates' behaviour rankle him.

"Why do you care so much about these assholes?" she said. "You're only here on a temporary basis anyway. You'll go back home in a few years. Just get what you can out of your time here and go!"

This really angered him. That Cynthia could feel so free to tell him that he would leave, that he didn't belong. That could not be. Nader had no plans to leave. He thought of the times he felt close to his roommates: that moment with Harv and the jogger, that moment when Jeff thought it was normal for Nader to have a girlfriend. They were small moments, but real. He thought of how ugly Cynthia was, to think he could be so ephemeral, so ready to disappear.

She was even uglier, actually; Nader had overlooked some things about her, but now they bore considering. She had an awful scar on the left side of her face, from some accident or something. Actually, it was a burn, poorly healed, that extended all the way down the left side of her body. An utter disfigurement. And she was callous. She lacked understanding. She was dirty. She was actually foreign herself, from somewhere horrible that she tried to hide. She probably even lurked at meetings of the International Students' Society. Perhaps she had even spent a night with Jeff, or someone like him, once they had both gotten sufficiently drunk. She was a disgrace.

IT WAS LATE when Nader finally walked back to the house. He saw that the light in the living room was still on. On other nights, he would have turned around and found somewhere else to be, waiting until his roommates went to bed. On this night, he didn't do that. He went inside.

"Well, well, well," said Jeff, looking up from the TV. He was smoking, his feet up on the coffee table. "If it isn't the man who's been avoiding us."

Harv sighed and scanned the room for his guitar.

"Let me guess," continued Jeff. "You've been at your fake girlfriend's place this whole time?"

"Jeff, please," said Harv. "It's too late at night for this."

"As a matter of fact," Nader said, "that's right, Jeff. I have been." He hung his coat and umbrella on the rack by the door.

"Oh, this should be good," said Jeff. "And what fake things did you fake lovebirds do today? Can't wait to hear all your stories."

Nader reached for an expression he had heard from Jeff before, an expression that he felt contained some violence. "I cut her loose," he said.

Nader felt a plunge of loss at the words, but he held his gaze steady at Jeff.

Jeff looked surprised. "Just like that?"

"Yeah, just like that. She wasn't worth it," Nader said.

Jeff sat up to attention. For a moment, it looked like he didn't know what to say. "Well, I guess no use wasting your time, right?" he managed finally.

The floorboards were loud underneath Nader as he entered the living room. He turned his back to his room-mates. It was an act of supreme confidence, something only an equal could pull off.

Nader looked out the window. The rainwater drifted down the street in runnels. He realized that, in the end, he had easily disposed of his problem, made it vanish into the sewers with the refuse and the squealing rats.

He felt a surge of power at the thought.

THE BODY

"I wish you would be excited for me," Sam pleaded. "This might mean I have a chance to make it—that *we* have a chance."

Joumana did not respond. She was always like this when something did not go exactly as she had planned. She'd play her echoey spa music and lock herself in the bathroom to paint her toenails or moisturize her neck or indulge in some other facet of her self-care routine, passive-aggressively separating herself from Sam in both mind and body. She'd said her piece, several pieces actually, and now Sam could bellow from behind the closed door all night and she wouldn't give him another word.

Not that Sam would *bellow*. There's not enough heat in their marriage for that. But to call his trip a vacation, as she did? It's a day or two in *Thunder Bay*, after all. Sam hadn't been to Thunder Bay, but the Google Images search—which he ran when he found out he would be flying there first thing in the morning—only turned up views of strip malls and traffic intersections. Aerial views at that, as if the helicopter photographers couldn't even be bothered to land for a few minutes.

He didn't tell Joumana this, but thinking about his trip gave Sam a guilty thrill. It made him feel like a television lawyer, taking urgent flights to solve impossible problems. The managing partner, Richard Pearl, said it himself: "This is not an assignment I can tell you how to do. From a legal perspective, it doesn't seem like there is anything we *can* do." Richard's fingers were interlaced on his belly at the time, and he seemed to be assessing the polish on his shiny tasselled loafers in lieu of looking at Sam. "If you're thinking that our client came to a law firm when they should've gone to some shady alleyway, maybe you're not the first one to have that thought."

Any of Sam's fellow students may have felt secure enough to tell Richard that they could not take on the assignment. *They are too comfortable*, Sam thought, *too unconcerned*. He, however, felt both privileged and relieved to have the opportunity.

"Can you at least tell me where you put my luggage?" he asked Joumana. The sound of the shower starting was his wife's only answer.

Sam's fight with Joumana—and now their silent détente—felt like a fitting end to an emotional roller coaster of a night. It had started at a fashionable club near the Financial District. The firm's cohort of students had been invited there for a night of socializing with the lawyers. The place was designed to get everyone to loosen up: there was a bar, a dance floor, Ping-Pong tables, booth seating, a holding pen of smokers defying the March chill out back.

But despite its veneer of casualness, the event was serious business for the students. It was their final chance to exhibit themselves. By the end of the week, the partners and associates would decide to whom they would offer permanent positions. The chosen few would be the newest inductees into the glittering society of the firm's powerful lawyers, and its rarefied clients. Their names, Sam thought with an aching desire, would be stencilled on the spotless glass of their own office doors.

As the firm told it, the work was the only basis for those decisions: how well the students executed their legal research assignments, their proofreading tasks, their document delivery errands.

"And if you believe that, I have a bridge to sell you in my bedroom," said Mia, Sam's only real friend among his peers. The two of them were standing by themselves, picking off canapés from the waiters walking by, and watching a spirited Ping-Pong match between colleagues whose suits were dampening with sweat. Mia's view was that everyone was more or less on an even plane as far as the so-called quality of work was concerned. "Really, the differentiator is going to be which of the partners or associates is willing to fight for you come decision day."

"But, for example, there's Caroline—" started Sam.

"Sure," said Mia, cutting him off, "Caroline is a genius, and it doesn't matter if anyone likes her. She's in, and she'll be a partner in no time, too. The rest of us actually have to sell ourselves, and find someone who will take us up on what we're selling."

Sam once had someone like that. Muneeb Alami. His name had felt so inviting in its Arabness when Sam encountered it while researching the firm prior to his interview. Sam reached out to him on LinkedIn, lowering himself to remarkable depths over just two introductory paragraphs. He signed off with his unshortened name: Sameer. Then he went ahead and wrote to just about every other lawyer in the firm as well.

None answered except Muneeb.

"Let's talk over a quick falafel tomorrow," he wrote, already treating Sam with easy informality. To Sam's delight, Muneeb turned out to be a star in the firm, the highest earner in the litigation group for two years running. All his cuffs were monogrammed in cursive, and his manner was as affable as the whitest of firm gentry.

Muneeb ensured the firm gave Sam a student position and took him under his wing. He involved Sam in numerous interesting projects and introduced him to other partners. Sam, in turn, dropped Muneeb's name into conversations whenever he could, using it like a mantle signifying his invulnerability.

But, only a few months after Sam's arrival, Muneeb left the firm to join one in New York. Despite having a warm goodbye coffee with his mentor, Sam felt abandoned. In the days after, some of the students actually approached him with condolences.

"I heard Muneeb is gone...I know you two were close," said Travis, chewing a protein bar at his desk, which adjoined Sam's in the student bullpen. Travis's father, a banking executive, belonged to the same golf club as half of the partners in the firm.

"Well, we weren't really that close," Sam responded.

Travis scrunched his eyebrows theatrically. "Wasn't Muneeb the one who got you here in the first place?"

"Travis, do you mind shutting up?" said Mia, from two desks away. "I'm trying to focus on these memorandum revisions. Thank you."

So this last party was critical indeed. Desperate for a new ally, Sam spent the night doing his best to make connections. Every time he saw a circle form around a potential decision maker, he tried to pierce its surface tension to insert himself among those whose status felt far more secure than his. Sometimes, one or two people in a circle even acknowledged him with a raised eyebrow. At one point, in an effort to appear busy as the conversation went on without him, Sam took out his phone and looked up the human muscle involved: corrugator supercilii. One or two of these corrugator supercilii in each circle would contract upon Sam's arrival, causing that narrow line of hairs to take a modest leap in his honour. Sam counted it a victory to have managed to move muscles that did not belong to him.

It amused Sam now to think of how acute his anxiety had been just a few hours before.

He opened the closet to look for his luggage. All he could find were Joumana's suitcases, a deep red set of three: "like our future family, inshallah," she had said in the hopeful first days. Although wary of upsetting her by taking one of her belongings on this disapproved-of trip, Sam reached for the carry-on anyway. It was still gleaming, immaculate.

He remembered the first time he'd seen those suitcases, the night Joumana arrived at their new condo post-marriage, heavy on eyeshadow and seemingly dipped in perfume. For his part, Sam's hair was slicked and parted sharply to one side, a last-minute attempt at a new hairstyle that he was certain had not succeeded. In a nervous attempt at lightheartedness, Sam had said, "Well, my dear, you look as good as you did in the catalogue." He quickly discovered that his new bride was not much for his brand of humour. That was also the first time Sam was introduced to Joumana's bathroom disappearances.

Sam now splayed open the carry-on and began adding items. The charcoal suit, for sure. Though it had been a sale item from a discount men's store, the most their family budget would allow, it would have to do. But once Sam landed a permanent position, watch how many sales clerks he would keep busy at Brooks Brothers. He hoped—somewhat childishly, he knew—that an upgraded wardrobe might make him more worthy of his wife's respect.

Sam could always tell that Joumana was in a foul mood when she brought the catalogue into an argument. "Why should you take into account the priorities of a girl you got from a catalogue, after all?" she'd asked earlier tonight. "Sure, these next two or three days that you'll be gallivanting in Thunder Bay will be your wife's most fertile days. And sure, that same wife is on so many fertility meds right now it's insane. Not to mention that for years she's sacrificed the whole idea of a vacation because we can't afford it. But why let any of that stop you? She's just a catalogue girl."

Now obviously it had not been a catalogue—not exactly. The whole thing had started when Sam was on the cusp of turning thirty. He was still a graduate student who had, until then, avoided any major life responsibilities, especially a wife. His mother, Adeela, finally realized that her years of generalized nagging about getting married had not made any progress with her son. So she tried a more direct approach: she began compiling an album of the marriageable daughters of her acquaintances and friends in the local Arab community. By the time she was done, she had at least two dozen profiles, arranged alphabetically. Each eligible bachelorette had her own page, which Adeela filled with printouts of photos she found on Facebook along with her own drawings of flowers and curlicues. On scraps of construction paper, she added for each woman a few biographical bullet points, which she had gleaned via some canny scouting at women's lunches and baby showers.

Sam finally relented when his mother shoved the thick album, which she called the Marriage Book, into his hands for what felt like the twentieth time. It was late at night, and Sam was eager for a half hour of TV before bed. After huffily leafing through it, he said, "Okay, we can think about this one." He handed the album back to his mother, open to a page showing a striking young woman with fair skin and shiny black hair. If Sam's memory served, the bullets relating to the selected woman read:

- Reasonable degree (M.Ed.)
- Great sense of humour

- Adventurous, happy to move
- Twin of Amal Alamuddin (hopefully with better marital judgement)

"Wonderful!" Adeela said, closing the album. "That is Joumana, the daughter of one of my very dearest friends, Nima. An excellent choice."

The meeting of the families took place on a Friday night, just after dinner. Sam and his mother arrived at Nima's doorstep bearing flowers and a box of baklava. Nima's husband, Irfan, opened the door and grasped Sam's hand in a firm shake. The smell of bakhoor, an incense of burnt wood, along with an underlayer of Dettol surface cleanser, swirled through the house. Sam was shepherded into the salon area and directed to a tufted armchair with a cartoonish gilt wooden frame. Irfan took an identical armchair nearby, and Adeela and Nima sat together on a matching sofa. A brass dallah was on the table before them, with a tower of porcelain demitasses near it to hold the spiced coffee. Sam felt like a foreign dignitary. The formality of the affair shocked and stiffened him.

After the initial pleasantries, a fact-finding interrogation was initiated by Irfan, whose daughter, Sam noticed, had not yet appeared. Sam was prompted to confirm that his father had passed several years ago, that he was almost finished his master's in physics, and that for now he worked part time as a TA. When Irfan asked him what he intended to do when his studies concluded, Sam's mother answered for him.

"He will be going to law school," she said.

Sam's stomach churned. Although he had spoken vaguely about such plans, he was still considering other options, including a Ph.D., or even some time off. Sam felt that his mother was adding new commitments to his life by the minute.

"Oh no!" exclaimed Nima, disappointed. "With your background, I thought you might continue with something like medicine, or engineering?"

"Certainly understandable, khalto. I suppose I just feel law may be more suitable for me," Sam said, forced to defend a career he had not yet chosen.

Irfan interceded. "Apologies, son. Nima just has bad memories of lawyers. We had a fence dispute with the neighbours a few years ago. There were very untrue things said about us in court. It was not a nice experience."

"Not nice at all," Nima agreed. "I can tell you the horror stories. But I guess lawyers are useful in these parts. Not like in our countries, where law doesn't matter and it's always about your wasta. That means having the right connections. You might not know that, having grown up here."

Actually, Sam knew enough about wasta. Many times, he'd witnessed his parents' relief when they had the right wasta to get something done in the Middle East. You need to land the right job? Hopefully you have a wasta, a strong enough relationship with someone well positioned to cut through the formalities (and worthier candidates) to get it for you. You need to force someone to sell you land? You better have a wasta. You need to get your cousin out of jail? Find a wasta. The power of wasta seemed almost mystical.

"Over there, no lawyer is as useful as a good wasta," Irfan affirmed.

This was when Joumana entered the room. Everyone pretended that her arrival was a normal thing—people enter rooms all the time. Only Adeela acknowledged, with an irrepressible smile, that this was the first time her son would see his future bride.

Immediately, however, Sam felt something was off. Joumana was certainly pretty, though Sam was surprised by her dyed blond hair, which did not seem to be a good match for her dusky complexion. Also, her cheek had a mole that he did not remember from her pictures. But she was dressed beautifully: a floor-length cream dress with shimmering fringes at the neck and hem, which Sam understood was intended to be form-fitting enough to catch his eye but flowing enough for their families to not think it immodest.

"Joumana, would you like to refresh our guests' coffee?" suggested Nima, thus granting her and Sam permission to have a closer look at each other.

Joumana picked up the brass dallah. She started with Adeela's demitasse, giving a warm smile as she filled it, and then pivoted gracefully towards Sam. He held his demitasse for her in the crook of his palm, as if he were awaiting alms. Joumana poured. As she leaned forward, her yellow hair, smelling sharply of lavender, hung in the air inches from him.

Sam was sure then. He tried in various ways throughout the night to surreptitiously get his mother's attention, but propriety and the geography of their hosts' salon made it impossible.

At one point, he and Joumana were allowed time to talk in private. This felt ridiculous, as they were both adults and could easily arrange to do so on their own, away from the prying eyes of their families. But they talked anyway, mostly about their educational backgrounds and careers. Joumana seemed perhaps a little on the serious side, but not unpleasant. She was remarkably sure of the plan she had for herself, and diligent about following it.

"If it were up to my parents, I would've been married when I turned twenty," she said. "But I was clear: university first, then pharmacy school, then a good job, *then* marriage. I turned thirty a few months ago, so it was time I let my mother start looking. I expect in two years I will have enough savings to invest in my own pharmacy and, hopefully, have children." Joumana looked directly at Sam as she spoke, almost challenging him to disagree with her path, before concluding, "I firmly believe a happy life doesn't just happen. You have to lay the groundwork for it."

Sam had to admit that, in a way, this strict adherence to a plan intrigued him, if only because it was so different from the aimlessness that had characterized his own life.

Sam and Adeela stayed late into the night. Every time one of them suggested they take their leave, Irfan and Nima insisted they visit longer.

In the car on their way home, Sam was finally free to let his frustration show. "This was not the woman in your book," he said.

"What do you mean?" asked his mother.

"Joumana was not the woman I wanted. Not even close."

When they arrived home, Sam fetched the Marriage Book and flipped to the bookmarked page. There, as he expected, on the left-hand side, was the woman he had selected, the Amal Alamuddin look-alike, someone named Janna. To his dismay, however, on the right-hand side was Joumana. About Joumana, his mother had written these bullet points:

- Wants someone capable and well established
- Ready for children immediately
- Too old for BS
- Daughter of one of my best friends — don't inquire if not serious

71

"I guess it was an honest mistake by both of us," Sam said to his mother, after he had calmed down. "Just a waste of a night. You will have to tell your friend it's not going to work out."

But Adeela was not willing to do that. The embarrassment of withdrawing interest after one meeting of the families would have caused an irreparable rift in her friendship with Nima. Instead, against Sam's protests, Adeela prevailed on him to attend at least one or two more family gatherings. Would it kill him to give Joumana a chance? Let's be realistic: Sam was not some kind of unmissable catch. He was a few years from middle age and still a student. He would be lucky to have someone of Joumana's calibre and beauty.

Six months later, Sam began his first year of law school. Four months after that, in the dead of winter, he was engaged to Joumana. They married the following June, in an outdoor wedding planned entirely by their mothers. It was a beautiful summer evening, with a refreshing breeze in the air. No one sweated; no one got cold. Afterwards, the newlyweds spent a week together in their new condo, before going on a honeymoon in Jordan, at a resort overlooking the sea.

Sam now placed two ties and two shirts in his suitcase. It had been three years since they married. For most of his time with Joumana, he was still a student, making negligible wages as a research assistant at the law school, and being supported almost entirely by his wife from her work as a junior pharmacist. He had not been the ideal plug-in for her life plan: she had to make significant adjustments to accommodate him, pinching pennies and putting on hold her dream to open her own pharmacy. Joumana treated Sam with affection, but these adjustments discomfited her. They lay beneath their moments of marital friction like termites under soft wood. Sam tried his best to make it up to her however he could, but he often felt he was several steps behind Joumana in their shared life, panting and tripping as he tried to keep up.

These days, their evenings, on the few occasions Sam wasn't working late at the firm, were formulaic: bagged frozen fish or chicken for dinner; a long absence in the bathroom for Joumana; episodes of competition TV programs involving food or metalwork for Sam. To cap the night, their procreational routine: the same brisk hand, the same last-second pull into her arid interior.

Except for today, when even this sad formula was replaced by their outright fight.

Sam directed his mind towards more pleasant thoughts. He remembered the expressions on everyone's faces at the party earlier that night when Richard Pearl strode to Sam's circle. Travis had been the star of that group, telling law school stories to a few nostalgic partners, interrupted only by Mia wisecracking at his expense. Yet Richard, for whom the circle opened effortlessly, went straight to Sam.

"Could I have a few minutes of your time?" he said, touching him on the elbow.

Wineglasses were halted mid-lift, mouths paused ajar.

Richard led Sam to a quiet part of the club, a lounge area for just the two of them. He sat down and motioned for Sam to do so as well. Sam smiled stupidly as he waited for Richard to speak. Richard crossed his legs. He took off his glasses and wiped them with a handkerchief from his breast pocket. Then he wiped the face of his phone and inspected it.

"Well, Sam," he said, "what I'm wondering is if you'd be willing to take on an assignment for me. It will be your last one as a student, as I know your contract ends soon."

"Of course!" Sam said. He could hardly believe he had been hand-picked by Richard Pearl himself.

"Thank you." Richard drew in close, the vest of his suit crumpling and his tie bulging. "Listen," he said, "I need you to smuggle a body out of the country."

Richard leaned back and breathed. He looked relieved to have unburdened himself.

SAM LEANED AGAINST one of the giant glass panels, facing away from the sun. The ground in Thunder Bay was covered in snow, and at noon, the glare rippling off it was intense. There were no chairs around him; the lobby of this government building was not meant for comfort. The best Sam could find was a horizontal support ledge built into the glass at knee height. He tried to lower himself to sit on it, almost fell off a few times, and then gave up and stood straight on his tired legs.

He glanced at the other side of the lobby, where the security guard was sitting. It had been easy for Sam to say, "I have documents to deliver to someone in this building." The guard waved him in without even looking in his direction, never mind asking for his name. Not much of a secure location, Sam thought.

Unfortunately, his progress stopped there. The building housed the Office of the Regional Coroner, but there was no directory listing the floors on which the various offices were located, and the elevator wouldn't lurch an inch without the swipe of an authorization card.

Sam opened the file in his hand. It held a single sheet of paper, which he had nearly memorized by now. A governmental form entitled "Certificate for Shipment of Body Outside the Province," partially filled out:

Re: Asim Beik_____, deceased.

I, _____, the coroner, do certify that I have investigated
the death of Asim Beik_____,
aged 27 , now lying at Bay Harbour Funeral Home___,
in the City of Thunder Bay_____, in the Province of Ontario, and
there exists no further reason for examination of the body.

The cause of death is as follows:
Natural causes___.

The body is free of communicable diseases:
Yes: X___ / No: ___.
(If no, the body must be reported to the medical officer of health.)

Date: _____
Coroner name and signature: _____,_____.

At first, Sam's task seemed quite simple, little more
than administrative. All he had to do was get this form
approved and signed. The usual procedure was to make a
request online or at a kiosk; sometime later, the coroner's
office would issue a response. But in this case, Richard had
told him, things had to happen very quickly, and there was
no time for all the bureaucracy.

"My understanding is that the family would like to get the body to their home country so they can perform the funeral rites themselves, in their traditional way," he said. "It's an admirable purpose, isn't it? You would understand that more than anybody."

The other complication was that it was unclear whether Asim Beik had, in fact, died of natural causes. Richard described a young man who had arrived in Canada three years ago as an international student, enrolled in the business program at the University of Toronto. The idea was to eventually return home and work his way up to taking over the family's considerable real estate concerns in the Middle East. Unfortunately, Asim fell into some suspect friendships, and his studies suffered. He was forced to transfer from one university to another, until he landed in the outpost of Thunder Bay.

"Perhaps he was unprepared for the shock of the freedoms we have here?" asked Richard, with a shrug of his shoulders. "In any event, that kind of lifestyle can lead to some accidents."

And so it was that, just last night, as Sam was navigating his circles, Asim's neighbours found him lying on the rosewood floor of his luxury rental residence in Thunder Bay, amid liquor bottles and drug paraphernalia. His short beard was stuck to a congealed puddle of blood that had seeped from his nose.

"The family's assumption—and I have no reason to doubt them; they are very good clients—is that young Asim fell victim to some terrible people who tricked him into trying such things." Sam gathered that the family wanted to avoid having the coroner's office conduct an autopsy. "That has the potential to get messy," continued Richard. "The family is understandably concerned about their reputation; they're very conservative. Plus, I imagine their businesses would suffer if news got out."

If Sam could get someone at the coroner's office to authorize the release of the body, the funeral home would be free to put Asim Beik on the first plane out of the country, to be received by his grieving family. Dead and cold, yes, but at least with his honour intact.

Sam had been too awed by Richard to consider whether what he was being asked to do was, strictly speaking, legal.

"Maybe this all seems questionable to you," Richard pre-empted, "and I understand that. But who's to say we're wrong? The boy had a nosebleed. That's all we know for sure. The family says he's prone to them. Add in the stress of his failing studies and life, and some type of physiological reaction is almost expected. Do we really need to root around any deeper than that?"

Sam now checked his messages, buying time before making his next move. On the airplane to Thunder Bay, he had sent several texts to Joumana, apologizing for accepting this assignment without consulting her. Usually, Joumana messaged back, at least to acknowledge him. But not today.

Sam looked at the elevators in front of him. He had been calling the coroner's office every ten minutes for almost two hours now. The first time, he spoke with a receptionist named Tanya, who connected him to one of the assistant coroners. That person, Ron, assured Sam that there was no way on earth that he could get the paperwork signed today, as this was definitely not the correct procedure.

"Number one, there's a waiting period," Ron said. "We can't issue any shipping certificate before that's over. Number two, for me to issue a certificate, I'd have to requisition a report from the death scene. I'm not just going to take your word for it. Number three—"

"But the family needs the body for, like, religious reasons," Sam interrupted, feeling even more pathetic than he sounded. "I'm just downstairs. I could come up, and we could be done in five minutes. Then it won't be your problem anymore."

"Not going to happen, sir. I suggest you stop asking. I don't know what you're doing here anyway. This building is not open to the public. You could be prosecuted." Ron hung up on him.

When Sam called the coroner's office again, he asked Tanya if she didn't mind connecting him to another assistant coroner. "Just not Ron, please," he said.

The next person he spoke to was named Romina. This time, Sam mentioned he was from a major law firm representing the family of the deceased, which he felt added a certain gravitas. Unmoved, Romina seemed to relish the opportunity to lecture him. She covered the same points as Ron but with less patience. She also said, "Is that clear?" following every phrase, which made Sam feel like a delinquent schoolboy.

After that, Tanya refused to connect him with anyone else.

Now that he was on the ground in Thunder Bay, Sam realized what his assignment really was: to get someone to disregard the procedure—the formidable, immutable procedure—for his sake. But why should they? He could not come up with an answer. He realized how meagre his legal education and training had been on this point.

He looked at his watch again: 1:30 p.m. A few individuals filtered into the building and waited for the elevator, returning to work from their lunch breaks. Sam considered sneaking in after one of them to see if he could find the coroner's office once he was on a floor. Maybe if he spoke with someone in person, he could convince them. Or maybe they'd take pity on him and help. But whom to sneak behind? The large middle-aged man in a curled polo shirt? What about the pair of young women, who may be too distracted chatting to notice him? Sam couldn't decide in time, and both opportunities passed.

The glare around Sam intensified as it refracted through the glass, and he shielded his face behind his jacket. Glancing down at his feet, he noticed that the sole of his right shoe had peeled again. The trail of dried glue glistened where he and Joumana had once collaborated on repairing it.

Against his every expectation, Sam had grown to love Joumana. He admired her decisiveness and self-knowledge. On most days, he thought his wife probably loved him, too. She knew that, despite his shortcomings, he was trying his best to help them reach the life she wanted. Today, he wondered if that love had been undone.

Sam's phone rang. Unknown number. He picked up, in case it was the coroner's office. "Yes, who is this?"

"It's Fred."

Sam had to think for a minute but then remembered the name. Fareed "Fred" Fahmi was a senior associate, going for partnership for the second time this year. Now that Muneeb was gone, Fred and Sam were the only Arabs left. Sam had tried to schedule an introductory coffee with Fred months ago, and although Fred had agreed, his enthusiasm didn't seem high. In the end, it never happened.

"Oh, hello, Fred. How are you?"

"I wanted to see how you're making out."

Richard had been clear that Sam's assignment was to remain extremely confidential. He even forbade Sam from taking notes; all he had given him was the form.

"With what?" Sam asked warily.

"The Thunder Bay thing."

"So you know about this?"

"Yes, Richard asked me to check up on your progress."

Fred had been made Sam's keeper, then. "I'm here. That's all so far," Sam said.

"Have you made contact with the coroner yet?"

"Yes, the assistant coroners, a few times."

"And?"

"They all say it can't be done. And now they've stopped taking my calls." Sam did not want to say that the more he thought about this task, the less proper it seemed. Instead, he tried to sound resolute. "I might have to be more... proactive."

"Do whatever you have to do. This is a critical client."

"I get it."

"We're talking very deep pockets. Developments all over. They used to be your old friend Muneeb's client. Responsible for a lot of revenue for us over the years."

"Oh," Sam said. "I wonder why a lawyer wasn't sent to do this then?"

Fred was quiet for a moment. Sam realized the question

was too bold, too flippant, for a student to be asking. But Fred answered him anyway.

"Well, Sam, I personally suggested your name to Richard. You know you're on the edge, right?"

"The edge?"

"Borderline decision, from what I've been hearing. They could take you or leave you. So I said, 'Let's give him a chance to prove himself.'"

It shook Sam to have the precariousness of his future employment confirmed. "I appreciate that you intervened for me like that."

"Can you call me when you have that paper signed, please?"

"Okay," Sam said. He added, "If it's possible to get it signed, I will do it."

"The client thinks it should be possible," Fred said. "Talk to you later."

Sam wished he could call Muneeb Alami. Even a brief, general chat with his old mentor usually made Sam feel more at ease and assured about his work. Before he left for New York, Muneeb had given him his personal number. But Sam did not feel he could turn to him on this, especially since it seemed like Sam was now expected to be the firm's new Muneeb, magically solving the idiosyncratic problems of those special clients.

Reaching out to Joumana for support was out of the question. Instead, Sam called Adeela, hoping that hearing his mother's voice would restore a sense of normalcy. But once she learned that Sam was in Thunder Bay, Adeela's social butterfly instincts kicked in. She worked to recall the names of friends who had moved there, and then tried to convince Sam to keep good relations by paying them his respects. The fuss Adeela made distressed Sam even more, and he quickly found a way to hang up.

Sam took a deep breath. The elevator doors opened and a woman appeared, about to exit. He ran towards her, waving at her to stop and mumbling about having lost his card. The woman reached back with her lanyard, swiping him in.

There were five floors. On each floor, Sam stuck his neck out just enough to read the names on the doors. He thought of all the distasteful things these people must have had to do in the course of their jobs; today was his turn to do the same. On the fourth floor, there was a large sign stating, "Office of the Regional Coroner," next to the provincial coat of arms. Sam hopped out.

The reception was a small beige room dominated by an old mahogany desk. A frizzy-haired woman sat behind it, pecking at a keyboard with two fingers and a thumb. Tanya looked up. "Can I help you?"

Sam once again explained what he needed. As he spoke, he realized he sounded childish and defeated. He didn't know what words to string together—in what ways to contort himself—in order to reach the simple, yet completely unreachable, thing he needed to continue to exist in the firm.

Tanya looked sympathetic but also disappointed. She made a phone call. Within seconds both Ron and Romina materialized at reception. In the harangue that followed, it was Romina who took the lead. Her face reddened with vexation as she recounted Sam's repeated transgressions. She tossed several hurtful adjectives at him to describe his behaviour, which he had to admit he deserved. As she spoke, Ron stood next to her, nodding. At one point, Romina demanded that Sam show identification, and he produced his business card, which was once an object of great pride, a marker of belonging to a prestigious firm. Now, as he surrendered it, it seemed like the final sign that he had lost.

The card stated that Sam was a student. Romina softened on seeing this. "I don't know who sent you here, but they shouldn't have," she said, walking Sam to the elevator. "Take this as a learning experience. I don't want to see you make this same request again. If you come back, you will be leaving with security, or possibly the police."

In the lobby, the sun had died down. Sam could see clearly in all directions, but all directions in Thunder Bay were depressing. He tried to distance the effects of the episode from himself: all that happened was that Asim

Beik would not be going back to his family, and his family would not be spared the ignominy of their son becoming a cautionary tale among their wealthy friends. Sam had a fleeting vision of Asim Beik's body, absurdly large and inflated, flailing above the Atlantic Ocean, his arms tied by ropes being pulled in opposite directions: towards the land in the west, towards the land in the east. But Sam knew that was too outlandish, even for a vision. The land in the west had won without any such dramatics.

Maybe life could be arranged the way Asim's family wanted over there, he thought, but over here, things operated differently.

He was tired. He wondered how long he could postpone calling Fred, and what he should tell him when he did. Sam strongly believed two contradictory things: that he had tried as hard as possible, but also that there was something else he could've done, though he did not know what.

Sam thought of his wife sorting pills into little jars at the pharmacy, cold with resentment for her husband and his useless trip. He looked at his phone. Only one new text, from Mia: *I don't know what happened in your meeting with Richard last night, but from the way you left in a hurry without talking to anyone, we all think you're either: a) fired, or b) now our boss. Please confirm a or b.*

He replied: *Definitely fired.*

A cab pulled around the corner, a layer of frost clouding the edges of its windows. As Sam moved towards the exit, he felt a hand on his shoulder.

It was Ron. Instead of a stern face, he now wore an enormous smile.

"Sameer, habeebi," he said. "Let me introduce myself again. I'm Raed. I saw your name on the business card, and it sounded familiar. Then it hit me. Your mother is Adeela, right? We know your family well from our days in Toronto. You have to come to dinner at my house tonight. My wife, Janna, is a great cook."

IN HIS YEARS with Joumana, Sam sometimes let himself imagine what it would have been like had he resisted his mother's pressure to get married. By now he would have been quite old by Arab standards to still be a bachelor, but very much a young man in the eyes of everyone else. He would be free to select someone well suited for him, someone he at least felt on an equal footing with.

What Sam had never imagined was what it would have been like to marry the woman he had actually selected (however disinterestedly) from his mother's Marriage Book. The woman from the left side of the page, the woman who looked like Amal Clooney, née Alamuddin. Yet tonight, in the unlikeliest of places, he sat down to dinner at this woman's round kitchen table, along with her husband, the assistant coroner.

Janna was beautiful, her skin smooth over the sharp lines of her bone structure, and her glossy black hair folded into a messy bun atop her head. She seemed cool to her husband, but positively overjoyed to have a guest to entertain, using her good dinnerware and cooking enough for many more than just the three of them.

Raed made a big show of telling Janna the story of Sam coming to the office and acting the role of a big-city lawyer. He chuckled as he recounted how, like an Arab mule, Sam had refused to take no for an answer, causing a huge commotion. Sam, pained but not wanting to be a bad guest, smiled along, even adding embellishments to the story.

Janna laughed at everything Sam said. Her thick eyebrows — her corrugator supercilii — shot up in excited anticipation whenever he started a sentence.

"Sorry I couldn't help you in the end, my friend," said Raed, as he concluded the story, "but you know we have procedures. My hands were tied."

"Oh, don't worry. I understand," Sam reassured him.

Raed and Janna inquired after Adeela, and Sam was only too happy to affirm that his mother was in good health and would be delighted to hear of this unexpected gathering. According to Janna, Adeela had been a fixture at every party that she had ever attended, someone she looked forward to spending time with. Talking about Sam's mother seemed to make Janna nostalgic. At one point, he glimpsed her tearing up as she ran to the kitchen on the pretext of refreshing everyone's water.

Sam had the ironic thought that, back in the Middle East, this couple's close connection to his mother—not to mention the seemingly fated way he had met them, even after ignoring Adeela's urging—would have made them the perfect wasta for him. His issue would have been resolved, no questions asked.

But here? There were procedures.

Sam asked his hosts what made them move all the way to Thunder Bay.

"Opportunity, basically," responded Raed. "I have a wonderful job here, perfect for me, great salary and interesting work. Real estate prices are good. Plus, Janna knows French, so they paid her more to come up here and teach in the high school." Raed gave a sigh of great satisfaction, as if living in this northern backwater had unquestionably been the best decision they had ever made.

"I keep asking you when we will go back," Janna said, folding her arms and looking down at the table. "It felt like an adventure in the beginning, but isn't three years up here enough?"

"Janna..." began her husband, but he didn't finish. Instead, he went over to where she was seated and hugged her, his torso covering her head. He gave an exaggerated moan of happiness. Then, proceeding as if this was all that needed to be done, he turned to Sam: "My friend, do you have an interest in hockey? The game is about to start."

They all moved to the living room. The sofa where Sam was invited to sit was recessed deeply from so many sittings. There was a team jersey hanging beside the TV.

"Oh!" Raed said, as if he'd just had a great idea—but all he did was excuse himself to go to the bathroom while the national anthems were being sung.

Sam felt awkward alone in the room with Janna. Luckily, his phone dinged. It was Joumana. The message said: *I got let go from my job at the pharmacy yesterday. I was upset and embarrassed, so I didn't tell you. I'm sorry. I hope your trip has been productive.*

The stab of guilt Sam felt was intense. He could've been at the airport now, trying to find a flight home to Joumana, instead of socializing with strangers in Thunder Bay. He immediately rose to leave, telling Janna that he had to go home to his wife.

Janna's eyes were sympathetic. "Wait," she said, and disappeared into one of the rooms.

She came back with a pen and a large stamp. "Here. Is this what you need to sign the paper?"

"Pardon me?" said Sam.

"Forget what Raed says about procedures. The kid is dead anyway. Who cares what land takes the body?"

Sam tried to understand. "You're saying you will sign the paper instead of Raed?"

Janna shook her head. "No. I'm saying I can show you what Raed's signature looks like, and *you* can sign. Then you can stamp it, so it's official. This is the stamp of the coroner's office, right here. Raed brings it home every day, for safety."

THE PLANE ARRIVED at the airport in Toronto at 7 a.m. It turned out that Sam could have stayed longer at Raed and Janna's house, as there was no return flight available until early the next day. No matter. Sam and Joumana had talked on the phone for a long time before he went to bed in the hotel. Joumana said that her employer had been very apologetic when he informed her that he would not renew her contract. He felt he had no choice: the son of one of his friends was freshly graduated from pharmacy school; if he denied him a job, the boy might be forced to return to China to seek work there.

Joumana understood. It was the way of the world. But it still hurt to be let go.

Sam had tried to console her by saying it was probably for the best. With Joumana's new-found freedom, and with

Sam's presumptive new job, they could look into getting a loan to open a pharmacy of Joumana's own. They talked about it uncertainly but with some excitement, like they were entering a new epoch of their lives together.

Sam now waited patiently with the other passengers for the pilot to allow them to get up from their seats. Even the flight attendant was still seated, her belt on.

Rules are rules.

Sam tried not to think about what he had done to complete his assignment. Instead, he steered his mind to the kid, Asim Beik, who was, after all, not much younger than Sam himself. He thought about Asim Beik's parents and family, who would at least experience some relief when the body of their child made it back home. He wondered if they would be able to gaze at Asim Beik's cold face. Would they embrace his body with theirs? Would they wonder how his time away from home had changed him? Would they forgive him?

Sam thought they would.

USHANKA

My littlest, my heart,
What a wonderful surprise to hear your voice on my messages! Sorry I didn't pick up to speak with you personally. The phone I have here gets so many wrong numbers. I've gotten tired of only managing a "Zdrasvutye" or a "Dobroe utro" to whoever is on the other side before having to confess to reaching the limits of my abilities. So I just don't answer anymore.

Habeebti, you don't even ask how I am? I know I've made everyone angry. I know you think my mind and sense are gone. But I am still your grandfather, in spite of it all. Have I not spent my life adoring you? From the moment you were a toddler, visiting me on the weekends, bouncing on my knee, your head tottering in happiness? Of course I love all of my grandchildren, but everyone could see that you, Dasha, were my favourite.

You know that when you were born, it was so unexpected. Your mother had long ago thrown away her maternity clothes and donated the high chair used by your older siblings. So when she found out about your imminent arrival, she and Fadel came to me and said, "Seedo, we feel this is a gift given to us to ease the pain of Sitto Durra's passing. We would be honoured if you named our baby for us."

"We are all mourning, my dears, but there is no reason to add years more of it by giving Durra's name to the new arrival," I told them. "Let this baby start fresh. If you agree, let's call her Dasha." The gift of God, according to the Greeks.

And yet now, my Dasha does not ask how I am surviving, all these miles away, in this foreign land. All she asks — all she *demands* — is: When will I stop putting the family through this? When will I come back?

Well, even if you didn't ask, I will tell you: I am doing fine. I got a good long-term rate on a clean hotel. (I won't say which hotel, in case your mother starts feeling heroic and books a flight to Moscow.) I am up to date with my medications. Actually, my diabetes feels much more manageable with all the exercise I've been getting. Rarely a day goes by when I don't walk for at least four or five hours, knocking on so many doors. And my joints seem to be enjoying the bitterly cold air.

This weather reminds me a lot of that first time I visited you and the family in Montreal. Your parents' application to bring me over had finally succeeded, and I was excited to come live with the Canadian branch of my progeny. What an introduction I had, the gust of cold wind walloping my bare head as I exited through the sliding doors at the airport. Until then, I'd spent my life first in balmy Palestine, and then in scorching Kuwait, so weather like this was a trauma. The chill felt like it would eat my skin raw. My moustache and eyebrows became families of icicles, and my nostrils filled with miniature frozen knives.

But you helped warm up those days, Dasha, coming back from university to wrap me in so many scarves like a mummy so you could take me on walks on Sainte-Catherine Street. I remember all the pit stops you had us make to warm up in your favourite used bookstores and bagel shops. You were so mature, even barely into your twenties, reciting your complex coffee orders and sitting cross-legged as you sipped.

Here, there are no bagels, but they have something called bublik, which is quite close.

That time in Montreal was more than a decade ago now; for someone your age, that must be like a lifetime.

You may not have any idea what I'm talking about, but do you remember that utterly perfect gift you gave me in my first year in Canada? As we were sitting with the family in front of the basement fireplace, you presented me with a beautiful grey ushanka, though you didn't know it was called that. It was a fur cap with flaps that could be pulled down to cover my ears and most of my cheeks. It was unbelievably luxurious and warm.

From that moment, I wore it every day I went out in those eight-month winters of ours. The whole family was tickled to see your aged Arab seedo wobbling down a Canadian street in a funny Russian hat. I have that very same ushanka here with me. I'm looking at it now as I dictate this email into the computer.

Dasha, I am fighting a lonely fight, if I'm being honest. I know you hate hearing this, but I am doing what I feel I need to do. I go around to all these wide, dun buildings— Soviet relics that they call panelkas—armed with nothing but a few memorized words and a crinkled black-and-white photograph. Anyone opens their door, I ask, "Vy videli etu zhenshchinu?" Have you seen this woman? I explain that she would be much older now, at least half a century older. I get a lot of brusque nyets. Some simply shut their door in my face without bothering to answer. A few have tried to help; we communicate mostly by mime.

So far, my efforts have not been fruitful, but I have a lot of ground to cover yet. There are a lot of panelkas in Moscow.

To answer your question, I would love to see your face, Dasha. I don't know how to call you with video, as you suggest, but I would be happy to learn. The only condition is that I don't want you, or anyone, to try to dissuade me from what I'm doing.

My best to you and the family. If you are still in touch with Georgiy, a tip of my ushanka to him, too.

Your Seedo,
Abu-Brahim

Seedo,
I can't, with this email of yours. I just can't.

Leaving aside for now how you, of all the people on this earth, have figured out how to dictate to a computer!

I want you to understand that everyone here has been worried sick about you. We had to take my mother — your *daughter*, who is now a senior citizen herself — to the hospital because she's been having intense stomach and back pains, which I am sure are entirely psychosomatic. And is it any surprise? You disappear from the house without any warning or explanation, and days later we get a text message saying, *I'm in Russia, looking for some woman, toodaloo!* And that's it. You didn't respond to the umpteen messages and phone calls we made, that everyone made.

We thought you were dead, Seedo. We thought you were kidnapped.

And now I get this email that sounds like someone sitting around with a pen to his lips, leisurely writing his memoirs. Who does this?

You didn't even answer any of the questions I asked you in the voice mails. Please focus for a moment and tell me:

1. Where are you staying? It's critical that we have a last known address. I shouldn't have to convince you of this.
2. Who is helping you? I simply do not accept that you are roaming around on your own out there. On your best days you tremble like a leaf — how could you possibly manage even something as simple as putting a key into a hotel room door? Seedo, please tell me: Is anyone keeping you against your will?
3. How is it possible you are up to date with your meds? Your doctor says you should have needed at least two prescription refills by now. Are you lying to me?

Please answer. If I mean anything to you, if you care about my mental health, you will tell me.

I won't ask when you are coming back, but do you have any concept of a plan? How do you see this unfolding?

I beg you to tell me that you aren't *actually* trying to find some Russian movie actress that you caught a fleeting glimpse of on the streets of Jaffa when you were a boy. Which, by the way, was over sixty years ago. The lady is for sure dead by now. If not dead, ancient. Those Eastern European women fall off a cliff around forty, from all the cigarettes and alcohol, if nothing else. And your film star would be several laps past that age.

That's enough for now. I don't want you to tire yourself looking at the computer.

Seedo, I love you so much. I'm so scared for you. Please, please, please let me send you a ticket home.

Love,

Dasha

P.S. I would prefer that you don't mention George again. I really hope you don't feel that my time with him makes what you're doing okay somehow...

My dear Dasha,

It's painful how you speak to me. But it's not your fault. Your mother, who means well, has for years shown you that I am someone who needs to be minded, who must have schedules kept for him and be carted from one carefully considered appointment to another. Someone who, if necessary, should be sternly corrected, like a boy misreading verses.

That's all right. God forgives.

I am sorry to hear that talking about Georgiy upsets you. I formed a good bond with that young man. Unfortunately, the family's reaction to him was really hysterical. It seems to me, us Palestinians can be even more insular than most. I tried my best with your mother, for whatever that was worth. "Imagine if Fadel had been a foreigner, a Russian like Georgiy, for example, and I tried to prevent you from marrying him?" I implored her. "How would you have reacted then?"

Of course your mother shot back that she wished I *had* prevented her from that marriage, and every marriage, so that she'd have been spared the betrayals of having children. You had her under some stress, let's say, at the time.

Still, I wish you and Georgiy had tried harder, Dasha. If I recall correctly, he was out of the picture less than a year or so after you introduced him to us?

I would like to correct your account of what happened in Yafa (not Jaffa—I refuse to write the name of my hometown in the way the British liked, my dear). To begin with, I was not a boy, but a man of almost seventeen. In those times, men that age got married and had children of their own, though your grandfather was a bachelor still.

Her name was Valeria Mikhailovna. I met her on March 15, 1947. It was a classic springtime dusk. The humidity had started to drain out of the air, ready to give way to a crisp evening. On those nights, my mother used to tell me to leave my bedroom window cracked while I slept, so that my dreams would have the fresh perfume of the sea.

But I was not heading anywhere near bed. I was at a café, having a cup of coffee before a night journey to Jerusalem. Back then, my uncle had a good business growing oranges on his many dunams of land, not far from the coast, in one of Yafa's suburbs. He let me work for him whenever I had time off from school. Mostly, I helped the farmers in the fields, but every now and then my uncle handed me the keys to the lorry so I could deliver baskets of produce to the port or to markets around Palestine. My eye was on a management job in the office with him for the following season, so I did anything he asked. I had taken classes at secondary school, and my English was good enough to even negotiate with foreign shippers if necessary.

The café I was in had no name. We just called it after its owner, a Christian named Abu-Daoud. It had a few chairs and backgammon tables outside under a canopy that was bowed from years of neighbourhood cats nestling atop it. But the real furniture was the men who sat at the café, each at their usual times and in their usual postures.

That season I cut a sharp figure, if I do say so myself. To look the part of a burgeoning citrus magnate, I had blown several months' wages on a suit that I asked a tailor to make for me. It was navy blue, with pinstripes and a wide lapel, made of virgin wool that hung on me as straight as a ruler. I wore it every day that I wasn't in the fields, topped with a keffiyeh and agal on my head. The men at Abu-Daoud's laughed and called me "Mayor" because of this getup, but I didn't care.

"Where are your eyes, Mayor?" a masonry owner named Abu-Mazen yelled out at me that night. He nodded his head towards a foreign-looking woman—pale skin, hemispherical cheekbones, auburn hair coiffed into a roll atop her head—who had entered the café, trailed by a gentleman.

There were a lot of foreigners flooding into Yafa in those days. Sometimes it was British emissaries and survey-ors sizing up neighbourhoods for their Partition Plan. But usually, it was more Jews freshly emigrated from Eastern Europe on the promise that they could take our land, either with His Majesty's permission or without. Every now and then, some of these foreigners stumbled into an Arab shop like Abu-Daoud's.

"Be serious," I said to Abu-Mazen, dismissing his comment with a purposeful slurp of my coffee.

Abu-Mazen pressed on: "Do you want me to teach you some Romanian so you can talk to her and maybe set your-self up with a Jewish wife? Any service at all for our Mayor."

This talk was in Arabic, but to our surprise it turned out the gentleman accompanying the woman understood us.

He murmured some explanations to her, then, switching to English and addressing us, he introduced himself as Dmitri something, and her as his wife, Valeria. He explained that they were in fact not Romanian, but Russian.

"And also, we are not Jews," he added.

"Oh, so you're pilgrims," I piped up, returning my empty cup to Abu-Daoud's counter, my suit buoying my confidence. The woman had taken a seat, with her knees locked together and angled to the side. Her skirt reached just to the top of her slender shins. "This is a long way from Bethlehem."

The woman turned her head and addressed me. "Not peelgrim, Mayor sir? More, to just...toureezm? In your country."

And those were her first words to me. I've not forgotten the way she said "peelgrim," in that deliberate, questioning accent she had.

It's strange how I still become a little breathless when speaking, or even thinking, about Valeria Mikhailovna.

Dasha, I'm sure you'll say the reason I'm breathless is because I'm old and tired. And maybe it is so. And, you are right on another front: I did not travel here to Moscow by myself. I took Iryna with me on this trip. Do you know Iryna? She was the home health care worker your mother hired to assist me on occasion, taking my blood pressure, staying on top of my medications and injections, and walking with me to various places. I had started applying for my visa to Russia a long time ago—you see, this was not some crackpot scheme I came up with on a whim—and I recruited Iryna to help me fill out the forms and such. When I told her my plan, she was quite worried about how I'd survive in Russia on my own. She threatened (though now she is adamant that it was not a "threat") to spoil my plan by telling the family.

I thought: Well, wouldn't it be good if Iryna, who is Ukrainian, came with me and helped me get around and talk to people? A duo is always better than a solo, as I have been telling you, and all my unmarried grandchildren, for years.

Lucky for me, Iryna accepted, and she is here now, on a paid basis. She's the one you have to thank for these well-typed emails (and for sourcing my medications from Muscovite pharmacies).

I now realize that without Iryna this whole expedition would have been unworkable. My plan had originally been to divide up the outskirts of Moscow, where Valeria told me her parents had once lived, into little areas. Then I would systematically visit the houses in those areas to ask after Valeria, crossing off the places I visited as I went along. There are...quite a lot of houses on the outskirts of Moscow. I knew that. In fact, when we arrived here and I told Iryna my plan, her jaw dropped, and she hit an old man rather hard in the arm (for some reason she had assumed I already had an address for Valeria). Iryna also showed me the proper pronunciation of some pretty advanced Slavic swear words.

But I told her: Politicians and religious people routinely go door to door. Why not me?

Unfortunately, I have discovered that most of these areas on the outskirts no longer include the estates that used to populate them. Instead, they're lined with rows and rows of these socialized housing panelkas, adding a kind of density I did not expect.

My plan didn't change much, but now I had to knock on a lot more doors, and climb many, many more stairs.

Anyway, I was talking about Yafa, but I got sidetracked. You know, on second thought, better that I continue in another email tomorrow. It's late here. I'm told I should lie down.

Seedo

Dear Seedo,
I'm sorry that I spoke to you disrespectfully. I didn't mean to. It was just the worry talking, which, yes, I do get from my mother.

You will always be my favourite person in the world. I hope you never forget that, even in your bumbling old age.

My turn to take a trip down memory lane. Do you remember those times at your shop in Kuwait, when I was a little girl? On weekends when my mom had things to do, she usually dropped me off at one of my aunts' houses to keep me busy. But I always begged her to let me go see you instead—in your Alhambra Women's Fashion Boutique, right in the middle of the bustle of the main commercial street.

The occasions when my mother gave in to my begging were the happiest of my childhood. I loved that long narrow store, with my elegant grandfather in his usual chair behind the cash desk at the end of it. (Where do you think I learned my habit of sitting cross-legged from?) I would spend the whole day ransacking the racks, making huge piles of what I thought were the most sophisticated dresses so I could try them on in the fitting rooms. I'd come out swimming in them, looking totally ludicrous, I'm sure. But you never laughed at me. You always gave me your views in such a serious way. "Well, my dear, I'm not sure the colour of this dress really highlights your green eyes as much as it should. Let's give more thought to the ruffled red one, perhaps?" I would burst into giggles every time.

And don't think I didn't notice that the women who came to browse the store always found a moment to glance at the ring finger of the gentleman proprietor in his fine suit.

I learned most of what I know about Palestine from you in the Alhambra Boutique. In the lulls between customers, you told me about your trips to Jerusalem on that bobbing

truck full of oranges: how you'd drop off the goods, steal
time for a quick prayer in Al-Aqsa, and then drive back to
Yafa in the dark to be ready for school the next morning. You
made similar trips to Nablus, Ramallah, and as far south as
Hebron. I remember how being called Mayor rankled you.
("A mayor would wear a tarboosh, anyway, and I could never
stomach one!" you said once.) When we huddled together
in the back of the store for a lunch of bread and yogurt and
tomatoes, you said how much better it would've been if
my late Sitto was setting it for us in the courtyard of your
family's old house in Yafa, surrounded in every direction by
the arched doorways that led to the rooms.

I remember you describing being driven out of that
house by the Haganah gangs in the middle of the night —
rifle at the back of your head, carrying only whatever
clothes you could fit into a small sack, with your mother's medicines and some pots. Even the pots had to be
discarded when they clumped you together like cattle
and made you board boats at the port, telling you to find
somewhere else to go. The whole city was emptied of its
Palestinians like that.

You always said you'd return some day, and you'd take
me with you. To me it seemed like a mission. You taught
me how to shake my shoulder just so, to make sure I'd
have all the moves for the day we would dance together
back on Yafa's salty soil.

I wish you were here with me, Seedo, so we could talk about all that again.

I will say that in all those conversations, I never heard about this Russian woman who seems to dominate your mind so much nowadays. Wait—you said you met her in '47? Wasn't that the year before you had to leave Yafa?

Listen, Seedo, of course I understand wanting to find someone special. It's been a long time since Sitto Durra passed, and you don't deserve to feel so lonely, even though you do have us around you all the time. Haven't we suggested Um-Othman, the widow of my father's friend Abu-Othman? She is so lovely, and she used to live in Kuwait, too, so you have that in common. Her mansaf is out of this world—I tasted it myself at the celebration for the birth of her first grandson. Best of all, she's so young, at least twenty years younger than you, old man. Total catch.

Seedo, it's been three days since your last email. You have to be in touch with me more regularly, or I will worry. Is everything okay? I sent you a link for a video chat on your phone several times now—not sure if you got it?

I'm glad Iryna is there with you. I'm guessing she reads these emails? If you do, Iryna, then I can't deny I'm disappointed that you didn't let us know of Abu-Brahim's plans, but I thank you for taking care of him overseas.

Dasha

Dasha,

Apologies. Iryna left me for a few days to visit some relatives near Kyiv. I thought it was only fair to let her do that, as she's come all this way for my benefit. But the poor soul had to take quite a circuitous route to Ukraine, on account of the current political climate. In the end, I was on my own for about a week.

Unfortunately, while Iryna was away I lost my phone. That's why you haven't heard from me. Nothing major, don't worry. I was outside, it was a bit nippy, and my hands were having one of their jitterbug days. I heard a ring, took the phone out of my pocket, and next thing I knew, it leapt out of my hand. Ended up sliding to the brim of an open manhole. I crouched down on the concrete to retrieve it ("God, no, don't!" I can hear you say), and the steam from the opening hit me in the face. There were some Cyrillic characters on the nearby cover that distracted me as I tried, for reading practice, to identify them. Anyway, I put my hand on the ground for support, and my elbow collapsed. I ended up swiping the phone right down the manhole by accident, almost falling in myself as I lunged after it.

An unimpressed police officer helped me up, saying some things in Russian that I couldn't quite catch. He took me to a nearby café, sat me down at a table, and brought over one of the patrons to scold me in English. "You lost, old man! You lost!" that person said to me, not knowing the multiple ways his broken words were fitting for my predicament.

But Iryna is back now, and so I am once again running on all cylinders.

I admit that without her, the search for Valeria Mikhailovna stalled. The unforgiving stairs in all those buildings became basically impossible. Instead, I opted to visit some other venues where Valeria might have left a trace. I went to the Russian Film Commission, the Expatriates Film Guild, the French Expatriates Association, and a few other circles and societies, to see if they had a Valeria Mikhailovna among their members or alumni.

The staunch monolingualism of the Russians is admirable, but unhelpful. I'm still not sure if the reception clerks even understood whether I was looking for someone, or trying to sell them something.

The other problem is that I don't have a last name for Valeria. The name Mikhailovna is what they call a patronymic—they are like us that way, they always carry their fathers in their names. (I assume Georgiy had a patronymic as well?)

In my one day of knowing her, I almost didn't get any part of Valeria's name at all. That's because after she addressed me in the café, I hurried out into the street before Abu-Mazen could open his mouth with more remarks. It was already late in the day, and I needed to complete my delivery.

I had left two neighbourhood boys in charge of guarding the baskets of oranges in the lorry. In those days, there were usually kids running around everywhere in old Yafa, ready to be assigned a task by anyone with a bald head and an air of authority (my head wasn't bald yet, but already there were signs of it). The boys were sitting on the rear fender where I left them. When they saw me, they quickly kicked a few orange peels under their feet and swallowed the rest of the fruit in their hands. I smiled and told them there was no need to hide. I paid them a small coin each for their time, and they scurried off.

That's when I heard her calling. "And how long do *I* have to sit with the lorry to get some oranges, Mayor?" It was Valeria. She had followed me outside.

As a teenager, I was frankly a little apprehensive about speaking to a woman, never mind a foreign, beautiful, married woman. "You can just have some," I mustered, and retrieved a couple, in their paper wrappers, from inside a covered basket. I noticed Dmitri was still engaged in conversation with the men at the café.

"Thank you. Do you have a knife, so I can peel?"

"Maybe." I patted around in my clothes.

"You know, Dmitri is not really my husband," she said. "We just say that because in Middle East . . . it's better."

I offered her my pocketknife. She took it and started walking down the slope towards the pier. "He is my director," she said. "I am trying to act in films in Paris. I have only small parts so far."

"We have a film theatre here in Yafa. The Alhambra Cinema," I said.

"They are not very excellent, the French films I am in. I think they will not show here."

"You never know, maybe they will," I replied. How could I have known then that the Alhambra Cinema would be bombed and shuttered before the end of the year?

Valeria and I sat on the pier's bicoloured stones, dry beige on top, brown with moisture below. I maintained a good distance from her, for decency in front of the eyes surrounding us. English was her third language, and my second, so we had to repeat ourselves many times to be understood. Valeria told me that her parents, who had been Social Democrats, left Russia shortly after the revolution. For them, it was an exile. They hopped around a few cities in Europe and settled in Paris. There they had Valeria, and no other children. I gathered that Valeria was about twenty-three or twenty-four.

After a few minutes, Dmitri appeared, clearing his throat to announce his presence. "It took me a while to find you, wife!" he said.

Valeria smiled at him and whispered a few words in French. Dmitri tapped a finger to his temple to acknowledge my having been let in on their barely guarded secret.

"These oranges are incredible," Valeria said. She had finished off the two that I'd handed her, without bothering to offer any to Dmitri.

"Thank you," I said. "They're from my family's orchards."

"Best thing I have had here," she said. "Dmitri's mother is from Lebanon. He told me stories about how good fruit is in these parts. He was right. It's like honey."

We sat on the Yafa pier and watched the sun finish setting.

"So you've enjoyed Palestine?" I asked them. The conversation was even more stilted with three of us.

"It's beautiful here," Valeria said. "But..."

"But what?"

"It feels like it's ... going? Like ... soon it will be no more like this. I don't know how to say it."

"Don't put too much stock in the news," I replied confidently. "We will never let this place go. It will always be like this, maybe a few changes, but not much. Yes, there are more Jews coming all the time, and lots of fighting for land. There was a farmhouse on an orange orchard not too far from here that the Jews blew up, which worried my uncle. And they destroyed the train station in Haifa, too, I heard. But it's all temporary. Things will settle down, and people will live together. Anyway, how can they get rid of us Arabs? It's impossible. What a sad dream for them to have."

I said those words. All of them. I was only a foolish boy of seventeen, but even seventy-year-olds talked like that at the time.

Valeria said something in Russian to Dmitri, who considered for a moment, and then told me: "She says that she is reminded of what her father used to tell her about Russia before the revolution. There were lots of protests, and some strikes. Battles here and there between Red and White. No one could predict for sure what would happen, but if you paid close attention to your country, you could feel things were changing. From little things, you could feel it. How people looked at each other. How they hated each other more loudly."

I don't know if Valeria Mikhailovna was trying to warn me, or just making an observation as a tourist. Either way, it seemed absurd to compare my Palestine to the cataclysm that was the Bolshevik Revolution in Russia.

We talked only a bit more after that. Valeria told me about her wish to go back to Russia one day, once the regime changed. She said her family used to have a small but lush estate just outside Moscow, where her father and his siblings played as children. The way her father told her about it so many times, it seemed magical, though she had never visited it.

A dacha, they call it.

"Maybe the dacha is like my own promised land," Valeria said. It was a bad joke, but I forgave her.

Sorry, my dear, but Iryna is again on my case to get some rest. I don't know why she is so insistent. All I do is speak, which I can manage for hours. There is no need for rest.

But I should be more understanding. I think Iryna has a few phone calls to enjoy with her relatives, now that she is so near to them.

Love,

Seedo

Seedo,

This new information from your story (which you are maddeningly giving to me in tiny little squeezes) has both clarified things and confused me more. The main question I have is: If this Valeria of yours was born in Paris, lived there, had a family and friends there, made films there, and took little touristy trips from there—if all that is true, should you not be looking for her in Paris, and not in Moscow? If I invested even half an hour researching, would I not be able to find her, or at least some information about her?

For sure this has occurred to you, Seedo. Has it not?

As for *my* Russian: yes, George has a patronymic. His full name is Georgiy Victorovich. You keep coming back to him, so I'll tell you what happened, even though it feels wrong to be involving my grandfather in my love life.

The family's reaction when I introduced George was insane, as you said, especially because I tried so hard to ease them into it. I had talked about how he was willing to convert, get married immediately, and have kids soon after. He had started taking Arabic classes and shyly tried out some phrases on my mother when he met her the one time. I did even more pathetic things, like getting you that ushanka (do I have the word right?) that you love so much. I found it at a crummy thrift store. It was made in China, but it looked vaguely Russian. I thought, "Maybe if Seedo is on my side I can make this work." You were always more open to other cultures than most in the family, and your word was always gold. I'm glad you love that thing, and I know you tried hard for me. But my mother was so adamant. It was sheer stupidity to think that headgear would change anything.

In the end, she wasn't what caused us to give up. Yes, part of it was that George got tired of being the bad guy, the problem. It wears on you, after a while. I understood that.

But it was more me. Remember our walks on Sainte-Catherine, you and me? Remember how, even then, in those bagel shops and smoked meat delis, you were still talking about us going together to Palestine, once it was free? Still blabbering about seeing your family's old villa near the seaside and tasting again from a true Palestinian orchard the famous "Jaffa" oranges that we would steadfastly boycott if we saw them at Whole Foods. Still saying the only thing you wanted from the world was to have Palestine's sun slap your forehead one final time before you died, with your children and grandchildren around you.

As unlikely as such a scenario was, I couldn't help thinking: How would George fit into this picture?

Could I imagine him being excited to step into your old house in Yafa? Would he understand the importance to us of that simple tray of bread and yogurt and tomatoes that we would lay out, as we sat together in the courtyard of our old family home?

What would George care about our nostalgia?

I guess it doesn't matter now. George has been gone for years. And has a Russian girlfriend, last I heard.

Meanwhile, it seems you've decided to never come back to Canada. This may have always been your plan. I see that, even as a married man, you named your old boutique after your fleeting moment with Valeria. Same with your granddaughter.

Dasha

Dasha, love of my heart,
You are mistaking my interest in Valeria for something like a lifelong disloyalty to Sitto Durra. Nothing could be further

from the truth. Despite my misery at having to leave Palestine, finding your grandmother in Kuwait was always the silver lining. My Durra was the pearl that I found when I was in the sea of exile. It would upset me if you thought anything else.

Let me tell you one final part of my story with Valeria. As we were saying our goodbyes, one of the boys I'd hired to guard my lorry careened past us at top speed, swiping the keffiyeh I was wearing clean off my head. In an instant, he had sprinted out of sight.

Abu-Mazen, the irritating mason from the café, was in the distance, laughing his head off. "Mayor of Russia doesn't need his keffiyeh!" he shouted at me, doubling over in laughter. He had paid the boy to do that.

I was mortified, and my hair was badly dishevelled. To her credit, Valeria pretended not to notice. She collected the discarded orange peels around us and walked with Dmitri to their car.

Still irritated, I got in the lorry and made the journey to Jerusalem, dropped off my baskets of oranges and prayed at Al-Aqsa. I drove back home to Yafa the same night, but later than usual. It was quite frigid by the time I was in my bed.

The next afternoon, I went back to Abu-Daoud's café. My hands were balled up in red-white fists, my mind full of many visions for how I would club Abu-Mazen. But he wasn't in his usual seat. I sat down and shouted out an order of Turkish coffee, but Abu-Daoud motioned for me to come with him behind the tall counter.

Abu-Daoud nodded to a small box, wrapped in smudgy newspaper pages. "The Russian woman brought it this morning," he said. "She told me to keep it safe until you came."

I forgot about Abu-Mazen and took the box home immediately. When I ripped it open, what did it contain?

A beautiful furred grey hat, with earflaps. My first ushanka.

Beneath the hat there was a note, written in cursive English script. "Mayor, this is for you, to replace your Arab hat. It used to belong to Dmitri, but I think you need it more. Good luck, and thank you for the oranges. Valeria Mikhailovna."

Valeria had also left a photo of her under the hat, something a movie star would do, I suppose.

I folded the photo and put it in my wallet. As for the ushanka, it was not one of the items I took with me when the militia came to my house a year later and pointed their rifles at my parents, my siblings, and me.

To answer your question: I wouldn't go to France, or look in France. You're right that in all likelihood Valeria continued to live her life there, content and comfortable. But the Valeria I would find in France is not the Valeria I want. Dasha, in all our stories over the years, I promised you Palestine. Valeria's parents, in all their stories, promised her Moscow. I had to see if someone, at least, had made good on their promises.

But that is neither here nor there now. I'm sorry to have to ask, Dasha, but can you come bring me home? I am ready. Iryna just informed me she can't help with my mission anymore. She has decided to return to her home in Kyiv permanently. She says our conversations showed her the way.

How can I blame her?

Seedo

AT THE BENEFIT

"Good evening. My name is Kasir. I am a refugee. I am here now, in my new country, and I am happy. But many are not lucky like me. I hope that from my story you will know how important it is to help the unlucky people."

Kasir flipped past this opening, the first in his slim folder. His language skills were now advanced enough that he no longer needed to resort to the one with the most basic words. Instead, he could choose any of the six different openings he had, which had all been ghostwritten for him by Mohsen.

As the emcee made his introductory remarks, Kasir surveyed the crowd of professionals in attendance. He imagined their wallets, distended like sated bellies, ready to open upon hearing him.

❧

"GOOD EVENING. My name is Kasir. Let me start by telling you what I left behind in my old country. I know you all follow the news, and have seen the images, but the reality is always much worse."

Kasir flipped past this one, too. Rafah, his town at the southern border of the Strip, seemed so far away now, he hardly felt connected to it. His uncles and aunts were still there, some elders, many cousins, but he rarely called them. What would he say? "Hello uncle, unlike you, I am well fed now, and my safety is no longer a continuous concern"?

No, the things Kasir remembered most about his old home were, strangely, connected to his cousin Mohsen. Mohsen had managed to emigrate as a young man long ago, establishing himself and starting a family. He returned to Gaza every few years—the ajnabi cousin, the foreigner— with his well-tended teeth and sunscreen-preserved skin, to make the rounds of his extended relations and lament his lost homeland. When he came, everyone knew to host Mohsen in their yards, the insides of their homes too shabby to subject him to for very long. Despite the wafting odours of animal droppings and stale bomb smoke, Mohsen acted like he was in paradise.

"How lucky you are," he would say, taking languorous looks around, "to still have our homeland's air cool the pupils of your eyes every day." But everyone in Mohsen's company would have traded places with him any day.

Kasir thought with disdain about how Mohsen's arrival was treated like Eid by his family. Upon seeing any of his uncles or cousins, Mohsen did the same thing: he spread his arms wide and took them into a close embrace, kissing each bristled cheek twice, and as he did so, he discreetly slid one hand into their thobe pocket to deposit there an envelope full of currency.

"For the family, for the family," he whispered over every charade of protest.

For the prouder relatives—the ones who refused to take his money, repeatedly pushing back Mohsen's hand with purposeful strength—he purchased one or two lambs each from the livestock market, instructing the seller to deliver them to those relatives only once Mohsen had departed the country. That way, they could not refuse what they clearly needed.

How easy it was for him, dropping in to hand out envelopes and lambs, Kasir used to think back then.

"GOOD EVENING. My name is Kasir. You may think that sponsorship of a refugee is too big of an undertaking for you. You may think: Can I really do this? I ask you: Think less. The lives of real people depend on you to extend your helping hand before counting the dollars in it."

The way Mohsen told it, and he told it many times, he received the call from one of his uncles late at night, as he was finishing his prayers. The static on the long-distance connection was bad. All Mohsen heard was "Your cousin has managed to cross the border."

"I didn't even know which cousin," Mohsen said. "But I dropped everything and began researching how to apply for asylum. For *whoever* it was." For emphasis, Mohsen flourished his arm through the air as though it were a sword.

Was Mohsen disappointed it was Kasir who had escaped? Kasir often wondered about that. Other cousins had less troublesome reputations: stoic, virtuous family men. Unlike the wayward Kasir. "Kasir byiksir," his relations in Rafah used to say, playing on his name: "The breaker breaks."

His father was arrested when Kasir was a child, held without charge for years, only to die in the enemy's prison. An ordinary life in the Strip. Since then, Kasir had not felt a strong need to follow the rules of those in power. Not that he did anything major: joining a protest that spiralled into a riot here, looting the mansion of a corrupt official there. Things Kasir felt he couldn't help doing. And the soldiers, well, those always deserved a licking, however you could get it in. If you could thump the back of a soldier's neck and run, wouldn't you?

There was nothing in Gaza for Kasir, other than the gravity of home. In between his frequent lock-ups, he worked odd jobs: mechanic, upholsterer's assistant, night driver on a friend's taxi. He resisted marrying anyone he might have to leave a widow like his mother. So when he had an opportunity to tunnel his way out to Egypt, he took it without worrying if he would make it, or if the world on the other side would be any better.

But, unexpectedly, Kasir's application for asylum in Canada was approved, on the strength of Mohsen acting as his sponsor. When Kasir materialized at Arrivals, thin and bedraggled, Mohsen and his teenaged son, Nas, were there to meet him. A feast in Kasir's honour awaited at Mohsen's house.

At the dinner table, Nas inspected Kasir in darting glances. "You have been to prison, ammi?" Nas said finally.

Kasir wondered, *Is that all they think of me?*

Mohsen intervened. "Nas, in our old country, prison is just the occupier's way of honouring you." He looked at Kasir for his reaction to this turn of phrase, but Kasir didn't respond. Only someone who had never known the enemy's indiscriminate reach would say something like that.

"Anyway, there's no cause for such honours here," added Mohsen with a laugh.

What Kasir remembered most about his first night in the new country was the dizziness he experienced every time he looked up at the vaulted ceilings, ribbed with gleaming wood beams, of Mohsen's suburban house.

"GOOD EVENING. My name is Kasir. I want to tell you about the three most important people to me. My mother and father are first and second, no doubt. They gave me life. The third is my sponsor. In a different way, he also gave me life."

Mohsen found Kasir a suitable apartment (which featured the marvel of an ensuite washer/dryer set), risked his impeccable credit rating as his guarantor, and procured for him donations of furniture. Mohsen sat with Kasir at the bank, making small talk with the clerk who opened an account for him. He gave him money (another envelope) for clothes and necessities. He showed him the best discount supermarkets.

He also secured for Kasir a job at his friend Amin's warehouse, where Nas also worked sometimes after school. The job was menial, but it would get him started. The first time he brought him to the warehouse, Mohsen clapped Kasir on the back and said, "You will prove yourself here in no time."

"It will be hard to stand out from the teenagers and the handicapped," Kasir replied, as his new co-workers shuffled by. In truth, Kasir was intimidated by their purposefulness, how they all seemed to know what to do, where to go.

Kasir could not deny how much effort Mohsen put in to help him, even if he disliked having to rely on him. In Rafah, Kasir had not relied on anyone, since everyone was living the same misery.

But Mohsen had slipped up, too, in ways Kasir had trouble forgetting. Mohsen had found Kasir an old Toyota that another of his friends wasn't using, and he invited him to come with him for a test drive. In the congestion of afternoon traffic, Kasir suddenly accelerated, trying to wedge himself in the space between two cars in front of him, to create a lane where there was none.

Mohsen gasped, clawing at the dashboard. "We don't drive that way here!" he cried. And then, in a lower voice, "It's like having another son," he said, as he rubbed circles into his forehead with the tips of his fingers.

"GOOD EVENING. My name is Kasir. When I came here, I hadn't had a steady job in years. In my old life, jobs were myths. Survival was day to day. Sometimes trucks carrying flour come, and they throw a sack at you. Sometimes you sell your things, until you have nothing more to sell. Sometimes you beg. Sometimes you do worse than begging. My sponsor helped me get out of all that."

Mohsen was not some sort of angel, safeguarding Kasir out of an innate benevolence. And Kasir resented Mohsen for pretending otherwise. When Kasir received in Mohsen's presence a phone call from home, Mohsen's ears pricked. If Kasir took his phone out of earshot, Mohsen devised excuses to wander nearby. He could almost hear his cousin thinking, *Is Kasir singing my praises? Do all the hajjis and hajjas know what I've done for him? Do they understand that I'm not just the rich ajnabi of the family?*

Kasir resisted being tethered to Mohsen. Gradually, he stopped showing up at community events, religious functions, most other gatherings. Mohsen barraged him with reminder texts and voice mails, to which Kasir replied days later, usually explaining that he had picked up some extra shifts at the warehouse.

"Why so many shifts?" asked Mohsen eventually. "Is it your apartment? We can find you a more comfortable place. I can give you a loan. The money you earn cannot be worth the sacrifice of never seeing you."

Kasir knew that Mohsen was offering a loan to avoid embarrassing him with outright charity, but even this consideration—which felt like charity in itself—rankled Kasir.

Mohsen continued. "What's wrong, cousin? I spoke to some of our uncles back home. They say they haven't heard from you either."

Mohsen seemed to be brandishing how much closer he had become to their extended family, closer than Kasir, who had spent all his life among them.

"I will call them," was all Kasir said.

He felt like an ajnabi cousin, too, now—except, a useless one.

A few weeks later, Mohsen came to Kasir with an idea. Mohsen said that he and some friends had started a foundation for refugees. He asked Kasir if he would like to come to its events, like fundraisers and benefits and such, to say a few words about his experience.

"We think it would be inspiring to hear a success story like yours," Mohsen said. "There would be an honorarium, of course, for your time," he added.

The thought of being paraded around like a prize fish grated on Kasir. But he couldn't very well refuse. The cause was good, and he had to admit, the money was helpful.

"GOOD EVENING. My name is Kasir. Let me get to the point. If you have a weak stomach, please turn away. I will lift my shirt now...What you see are the marks my old country left on me. The longitudinal scars here are from when a soldier lashed me with the muzzle of his rifle, as his colleagues pinned me by my limbs. It was sharp, that rifle, like the soldier had ground the tip down for an occasion just like that. And these two grey circles near my shoulder (sorry, I have to lift my shirt up more) are from rubber bullets. You can see what they looked like when they were fresh, up there in the photograph on the screen."

In recent times, this was the opening that Kasir used most. He found its bluntness satisfying, both in its words and in the unforgettable exposure of his mangled torso. It made him feel different from his pampered audience. His audience of would-be Mohsens.

But if Kasir lifted his shirt on this day, his old scars would be overshadowed by fresh wounds. Last night, the warehouse manager spotted Kasir trespassing in the owner Amin's office. The manager rushed towards Kasir, yelling, "Hey! What're you doing?" Kasir cocked his arm back reflexively, like he used to do at enemy soldiers. Each man fired a volley before both of them fell to the ground, flailing at each other. Kasir wished he could blind the manager with his punches, but he was soon pinned by the larger man.

The commotion brought several workers to the scene. Nas, who happened to be on shift, called his father.

Later, at Mohsen's house, Kasir was given a fresh shirt and dressings for the lacerations that pulsed on his body.

"I did not steal anything from that box," he said, without looking at Mohsen. "Nor was I going to."

"Of course, of course," Mohsen replied. "I believe you, cousin. This is just a misunderstanding." When Mohsen's phone warbled minutes later, he jumped to answer it, retreating to another room.

Kasir sat in the living room, alone. He was not a citizen yet. Deportation was very possible should he be arrested and convicted. He looked up. The majesty of the vaulted ceiling felt humbling, and humiliating. The power in those soaring lines, their reach and symmetry. And this wasn't even some mosque or church or temple. It was just a man's home.

At this, Kasir's memory, like an obnoxious friend, brought him back to one of Mohsen's visits to his house in Rafah years ago. Kasir had butchered a sheep for the occasion, over his cousin's protests. ("It's one of your herd anyway," he had said dryly to Mohsen at the time.) As they ate dinner together, Mohsen asked, "Is there anything I can do for you, cousin?" It was a common nicety, but as he said it, Mohsen looked deep into Kasir's eyes, like he was begging to be allowed to help. Kasir was struck by Mohsen's desperation; he did not understand it. Of course he said no. Later, when they went inside for evening prayers, pieces of rotted brick fell from Kasir's living room ceiling, crumbling on their heads and prayer mats.

Mohsen now came back from the other room, relief stark on his face. "Amin and I came to an agreement," he said. "Amin will figure out the amount that is missing from the petty cash box, and I will pay it. In exchange,

Amin will not file a police report. We will also have to find you a new job."

Quietly, Kasir reiterated that he hadn't taken anything from the box.

"Really, it doesn't matter," Mohsen said. "The important thing is for this situation to not get any worse. So I will pay and take care of it."

"Okay, if that's what you think is wise," Kasir said. "You know how this place works better than I do."

Mohsen and Kasir looked at each other for a moment, neither saying anything. Kasir felt that Mohsen wanted some small show of gratitude from him, something. But Kasir could not give it.

"Anyway, before you go to sleep tonight, be sure to put some antibiotic cream on that cut on your forehead," Mohsen said eventually. "We have the benefit tomorrow."

AFTER KASIR DELIVERED his speech, volunteers from the foundation solicited donations. Many large amounts were announced on the spot, to great applause for the generous donors. Dozens of donation cards were also collected, from those who preferred their gifts remain anonymous. A few people even pledged to sponsor refugees themselves. Those declarations brought the biggest cheers and many handshakes.

Afterwards, a traditional band came onstage to play. A baritone oud, a tabla, and singers in braids and embroidered dresses.

Kasir left before the music started. Outside the doors of the events hall, he couldn't remember what opening he had selected on this night. It didn't matter. He had played the part of the grateful refugee well. He vividly represented the suffering in his old country. That was what was required of him.

But he knew that the people back home in Rafah did not think of him as one of them, really, not anymore.

In his studio apartment, Kasir turned on the lights, which flickered momentarily. He drank a glass of water, slumped at his small kitchen table. There were several envelopes arrayed there. Handwritten on each of them was the name of one of his uncles or cousins back home. The envelopes felt light, but less light with tonight's honorarium, and yesterday's petty cash.

The lamp above him flickered again. The ceilings in this apartment were low, Kasir thought, but not close to crumbling.

WOODLAND

Shareef was the one who took me to my first auction in the country. When we were first messaging he even suggested we meet at one. I wrote back, *What would a girl like me want with old junk? I'm an artist, I create new things.* At the time, I was trying to convince myself that this was true.

We went to a small gallery downtown on Dundas Street for our first date. He took pictures of my bemused smile and big Amazigh hair next to several works of mixed media.

For our second date, he took me to an auction in Stouffville. I thought, *How small can a town be?* We were in a community centre hall with yellow-stained drop ceilings. At the registration desk there was a pair of metal coffee Thermoses, regular and decaf, unlabelled. I think you were meant to know which was which by the sides of the table they were on. Elderly people in khaki shorts and oversized, shapeless frocks held their cups close to their mouths, ready to drink once they finished speaking to one another.

"Most of these auctions are made up of estates that need to be liquidated," Shareef explained as we made our way through the display tables. "When someone dies, all their friends gather to see if they can buy the things they had their eye on while the person was alive."

In spite of his city-tight pants and dark skin, Shareef seemed in his element there. He went through the auction with painstaking thoroughness, inspecting everything: rusted metal canisters, wooden golf clubs, patinated stepping stools, washboards, Royal Doulton figurines (chipped and unchipped), pocket watches with silver chains, amateur watercolours by unknown retirees, old egg crates that could hold books, silverware sets that you had to count to be sure were complete, snow globes, snowshoes, licence plate collections, Margaret Laurence paperbacks, tractor parts clogged with hardened soil, rotary telephones, push-button telephones, vases, cameras with leather carrying cases, decorative sinks, sinks so ugly that they could be decorative—seemingly anything aged and tactile and dirty.

Shareef struck up conversations with other auction goers, and within a minute, he was slapping their backs like a friend, or guffawing and pointing at them after they made a joke.

"Yes, exactly, like *Omar* Sharif," he'd say to the old white men and women. And "I'll be seeing you at the bridge table if you're not careful."

The dust from the inventory caused me to cough a lot, but I couldn't help but be charmed by Shareef's comfort in his surroundings. At one point, he turned to me and asked quite seriously if I wanted anything from the snack kiosk. All it had were skinny hot dogs revolving on a roller and Snickers bars in faded wrappers.

We didn't buy anything at that auction. I played at pushing Shareef's hand down every time he tried to raise his numbered paddle to bid on something.

Two days later, he texted me a video of himself imitating me by coughing exaggeratedly into a flowered shawl, stifling a smile.

Hey, that's my *shawl!* I texted back.

You forgot it in my car, he wrote. *I'm glad I didn't leave the auction empty-handed after all.*

I replayed the video several times, admiring Shareef's smooth, veined arms holding my garment.

There were many more country auctions for us. Old people never stopped dying, it seemed. We went to places like Uxbridge, Waterdown, New Tecumseth, where the land seemed so flat, I imagined you would not only know all your neighbours, you could practically see them everywhere on the horizon. Whenever Shareef was considering a bid on some grimy curio or other, he'd ask my opinion, wanting me to marvel as he marvelled. I twisted my face into incredulous knots at him.

"Stop trying to buy a past that belongs to other people," I said.

He laughed. "A bit rude to say that to a Palestinian," he answered.

I admit I also found some enjoyment in those auctions, in seeing—from the farness that I felt in myself—the townsfolk congregating, their good-natured bidding. A wrinkle of reserved joy, perhaps even some pride, materialized in each of their faces when they captured an item.

Afterwards, Shareef and I often looked for a bit of wilderness to explore in the surrounding areas. Sometimes what we found was barely more than a copse, cut by a trail. But those were my favourite times, just Shareef and me in the din-free air, our only company the brush, the water, and the creatures lurking within them.

At an auction in Bolton we saw on offer some limited edition prints of Indigenous art: bright, elemental depictions of wolves and birds and bears and humans. They shone like embers amid the drabness of commonplace Canadiana.

"Those are by Norval Morrisseau," I said. "He's a famous artist of what's called the Woodlands style." My first year Painting professor at OCAD had dismissed this kind of art as "primitive, traditional designs about things like spirituality and healing and such." It reminded me of the way Arabs in Algeria spoke of my grandmother's Kabyle tattoos, or her embroidery.

Shareef nodded, gazing at the prints in appreciation. "I see a lot of Morrisseau's stuff at auctions. One day, if I have the chance, I would love to buy one of his originals."

I yearned for my own art to have anything like that effect on people. I had let go of a job in marketing to become an artist and was starting to worry that I'd made a major mistake. With graduation from OCAD a few months behind me, I lived in a basement apartment near the railroad tracks in the Junction, surrounded by peeling paint (not the artful variety) and, on rainy days, the smell of mould. I filled my days by experimenting with various projects, and then destroying them in frustration soon after starting. To stay afloat, I wrote copy on a freelance basis.

I wondered if Shareef, with his practical job on the fund-raising team of a local hospital, ever questioned the sanity of what I had done. Instead, he seemed to derive a proximate thrill from it. He peppered me with questions about my inspiration (almost gone after my first two years at OCAD), my process (as if I had any), and my dreams (mainly, avoiding the bankruptcy that, from looking at my depleted savings, seemed imminent).

Once, an outdoor auction in King City was cancelled due to rain just as we arrived, so instead we drove to the

McMichael Gallery, a museum on Ojibwe land, in the middle of a nature reserve in Kleinburg. The museum had a sizable collection of Morrisseaus.

We stood transfixed by one in particular—a large, variegated canvas. I said there were rumours that the artist's relatives forged his work, selling it at auctions to buyers pining to display a token like that in their homes.

"I'm not an artist myself," Shareef said with a shrug, "but it seems to me there are worse things than having your work become the family business."

"You're right," I said. "You're not an artist."

At my place that afternoon I asked Shareef if he would be my model. I was mostly a painter, but I had a basic SLR camera. I told him to hold my childhood blanket and close his eyes. My high basement window was above his head, alight with sun. I called the picture *Shareef cradling something of me that predates him*.

Most evenings, I went for a run. I'm not a natural runner, unlike Shareef, but I am a natural escapee. I run almost with my eyes closed, imagining that I am fleeing to the mountains of North Africa—my home—with my hair travelling behind me like a streak.

Shareef ran with me a few times, but he was either too fleet, or brought me back from my mountains with his chatter. I said maybe this could be something we did separately. Anyway, I think he preferred the afternoon running group he found. He could've led the way every time, but took to settling in the middle, shouting jokes at those in the front and urging on those in the back.

I made more pieces with Shareef. I photographed him leaning against my old aquamarine bike, or holding up Polaroids of my parents dancing with teacups and saucers in their hands, or hugging to his chest the trinket-bedecked wedding dress from my old marriage, which I had offered for sale online for months without success.

Sometimes I underlaid those pictures with rough-cut drawings of mountains that I found on the internet. Sometimes I painted the mountains myself. The series grew extensive.

Creating these pieces felt dangerous, intertwining Shareef and me together like that.

It also made me think of my home, and the mess I'd left in my wake. My husband, suddenly bereft of a fresh bride, one whose tagine was irreparably bad but who had a lot of youth left. My father, no doubt regretful for permitting his daughter a measure of independence in the form of a higher education at l'université de Tizi Ouzou. My brothers, so incensed by their little sister's gall in simply *leaving*, as if that were a decision that affected no one but her. And my mother, unaware that I had left because she beat me to it, abandoning us for America when I was a small child.

Most of all, I thought of the mountains that hugged our tiny village, that circumscribed our world. I missed those mountains, even if I always longed to escape their embrace.

Another picture that Shareef sent me: a menagerie of all the pieces he'd purchased on our auction trips. He had gathered them on his dresser, arranged from littlest (a pair of brass bookends shaped like loons) to largest (a pre-1948 globe on a stand— "a commonly desired item for my people," he said).

Just send me a picture of your face, I messaged back. *It's better than all of those things.*

I entered two pieces from my Shareef series into a show that OCAD put on to display the work of recent graduates. Encouraged by this, Shareef brought his late mother's wedding dress to my basement. He laid it on the back of my sofa and asked me to pose next to it, admiring its bright red tatreez. "Monkey see, monkey do," he said, as he took my picture.

I resolved to try to accept Shareef's love. "Don't call my boyfriend a monkey," I said. "He's just odd, that's all."

UNLIKE THE MEN before him, Shareef overwhelmed me with his availability. I was still getting used to the terrifying vacancies of my new life. Without a regular job, every day was an open vista of: 1) creative possibility, but also, 2) potential failure. Shareef helped fill those spaces. His presence — speaking to me as if I were a reasonable, comprehensible person — made what I had done seem like less of a catastrophe.

I preferred seeing Shareef at my austere subterranean apartment. His place was close by, a well-appointed condo in Bloor West Village, with a concierge who was lax but, in general, awake. A proper dwelling, yet I could not tolerate it. The droves of auction finds were the least of it. Every inch of his place was covered with photographs of every relation and friend he had ever had, often from multiple points in their lives. Many were pinned to the wall with thumbtacks, the snaps having propagated at a pace faster than Shareef's ability to buy frames for them.

Shareef's family was all back in the Middle East, concentrated in Abu Dhabi. At least once a day, he checked in on each of his four siblings, the eldest brother assuming the role of his deceased parents.

"I forgot to call Eesa today!" he exclaimed once as he woke up from a Sunday nap, jumping frantically from the sofa and checking the time to see if it was too late.

I wondered, *Would the world stop if Shareef did not make his phone calls?*

A frequent sight: Shareef at the kitchen counter, chopping ingredients or stirring a pot for dinner, while one of his sisters kept him company on a laptop screen, her excitable Arabic breaking up every now and then over a bad connection.

"Why don't you pop your face on camera to say hi to my family sometime?" he asked me after one such call.

When I didn't want to discuss something, I answered in French, which he barely understood. "Peut-être un jour," I said. "Mais écoutes—you don't have to make us dinner every day like this. We can just skip it. God knows my pants wouldn't mind."

But I was not the only one who had a say in his cooking. My landlady, an old, narrow-faced woman, lived in the main house above my basement. My interactions with her had always been businesslike, but after Shareef began making meals at my place, I noticed that she often found occasion to shuffle her feet in the backyard outside my basement window, humming happily. Once or twice she said aloud, to no one, "My, what a wonderful aroma!"

Shareef began bringing her a portion of our food. "Eileen is a widow, Noor," he informed me. "She says she hardly ever eats proper meals since her husband passed away last year. 'Who is there to cook for anymore?' she said. It broke my heart."

As a result of this break in Shareef's very large heart, I felt I now had another person who was too aware of me.

My cocoon with Shareef was always more crowded than I wanted.

At night, without our clothes, Shareef was industrious. He always got me *almost* there. But any glint of a car's headlights that escaped through the blinds, or faint sound of neighbours' footsteps returning home, was fatal. All I could do was pull Shareef's face up and settle his breathing on my perspiration-covered chest.

Even on the joyous night when I received the news that my two pieces from the OCAD show had sold on the spot, we could not make it happen. The faces on his walls had become burned into my memory, and they materialized whenever we were alone together. My mind was overrun by all the eyes that I felt were looking at us.

"It appears I'm distracted by my new status as a paid professional artist," I joked. It was after midnight, but I pulled on a hoodie and a pair of leggings and went out for a run.

When I left for Canada, I severed all my contacts in Algeria. I didn't tell anyone where I was going, which country or even which continent. But on my night runs, I imagined members of my family in the silhouettes darkening the lit windows that I passed. I imagined them looking at me and wondering at the lunacy of this galloping woman. "Is she not cold?" "Is it not too late?" "Is she not afraid of what can happen to her in the dark?" "How dare she?"

. Shareef asked me once: "What were you running away from?"

I told him: no one abused me, no one mistreated me, no ghosts chased me. I just did not want what I had there — the script for my life, for how and with whom it was supposed to unfold until I died. Was I the first one to pine for the freedom, the tingling uncertainty, of being alone in a new world? Why can't a woman just leave?

I had resisted meeting Shareef's friends a few times, but eventually I had to relent. He made a reservation at a restaurant on the most bustling part of King Street, one of those places that combined two improbably paired cuisines. It was dark, loud, and ostentatiously casual, as if it were trying to convince us of how natural the fusion was. The hostess was wearing a brand of jeans that I used to represent. Shareef's oldest friends, two newer friends from his running group, and one of his cousins were all there, enmeshed by Shareef. I had flashbacks to my old job, and my old marriage — all the life it took out of me to be enjoyable to people.

Shareef clinked his glass with a fork. "Can you believe that, thanks to Noor's artistry, this face of mine has now been inflicted on at least two homes in Canada? Probably given pride of place, even!" His friends chortled and whistled. "But seriously — and, Noor, I hope you don't mind if I steal your thunder on this one — her pieces were so well regarded, and caused such a ruckus in the art community, that she has been asked to hold a solo exhibition. One of the university's major patrons offered to put it on. You will all be there, and it will be incredible."

At home, in bed together, I visualized Shareef with me in the pockets of North Africa's forests, high, high above. The dense trees below us looked like clumps of cotton, like thick, verdant curls. He called me Noora, like my family did when I was a child. I wanted to forge ahead.

On doit aller plus loin, I said. But he did not listen.

Let's go back to the village, Noora, he said. *I want to meet your father.*

Non, Shareef! Je veux que ca soit seulement nous deux. Je veux te montrer les montagnes.

I pulled him back up to me—it was no use, again—and let myself sleep.

The next day Shareef suggested we get out of the city. "Don't tell me there's another auction," I said, too quickly.

He was unperturbed. "Well, if you're not interested in an auction, what do you think about going to a cottage for a weekend? Eileen said she has a place about three hours north of here that's gone unused since her husband passed. Poor woman has arthritis and no kids to help. No way she could manage it on her own. She said she'd love for us to go visit, make sure things are still okay up there."

"I've never been to a cottage," I said.

"Oh, then we *have* to go. It's one of those quintessential things they do in this country. They build shacks in the middle of nowhere, surrounded by woods and water. In the summers they go there and do nothing but canoe and play board games and drink. You don't think you'd like it, until you go once and fall in love."

"Let's see how my show turns out," I said. "Then we can think about it."

My show was, without question, a great success. It was composed entirely of my Shareef pieces, held at the same gallery where we first met. Curators, agents, collectors, students — all attended, flitting from piece to piece, oohing and hushing. Shareef invited many of the affluent families he had formed connections with from his fundraising job, and many brought their affluent friends.

Dressed in a dashing smoking jacket, Shareef did not leave my side, receiving with grace people from the art community that I should've recognized but did not. Even though he was on the walls everywhere around us, he gently batted away comments about his stardom, deflecting the credit back on me.

A former professor of mine approached us in her pink heels, aperitif in hand. "Eloquent work, Noor, truly. Everyone I've spoken to has been so impressed by all of this...the love, the bittersweetness, the longing to fit Shareef into your world. But I was wondering: Have you considered perhaps doing a parallel series, switching your roles? Him behind the camera, you in front of it posing with elements from *his* past? It would seem to be such a natural progression."

"That's what I keep telling her!" Shareef interjected. "But I don't think she likes my things anywhere near her." He laughed.

Most of my pieces sold, each for several thousand dollars.

THE EXHIBITION TOOK place in late September. Soon after, I walked upstairs to Eileen's door and rang the bell. Her eyes widened in surprise when she saw me.

"Noor, it's you! I thought it might be your sweet gentleman friend," she said. "How are you?"

I said everything all at once: "Eileen, hello. I'm sorry to disturb you. I'm here because I would like to stop living in the basement. I know I should give more notice, but I would like this month to be my last one. Having said that, would you be interested in letting me rent your cottage?"

Eileen shook her head as if trying to expel something from it. She muttered that although the cottage was winterized, it really wasn't the right season for enjoying it as it should be enjoyed. I told her that didn't matter to me.

"Well, as long as you're okay with getting a bit chilly out there in front of the lake," she said. "I guess just let me know which weekend you want to book."

I said I wanted it for a year.

Later, when I told Shareef that I was leaving, I lied and said I was going back to Algeria to live with my family, and that I didn't want him to come with me.

His face yellowed with sadness. He asked: had he done something wrong, how long had I known, did I think I might reconsider, did I think I might return?

I had no real answers to any of his questions.

Over that last month, I packed just two bags: one for my clothes, one for art supplies. Most of my things I sold or left on the sidewalk to be claimed by the neighbourhood or the trash collectors.

We spent all of our remaining time together at his place, trying to avoid discussing my decision. On the one occasion when he, dutiful though half-hearted, attempted to pleasure me, I orgasmed within a few minutes. In light of the circumstances, I kept as quiet as I could, and shrank into myself with shame.

THE COTTAGE WAS located on White Lake, in the Kawarthas. Eileen said it was about forty-five minutes north of Bobcaygeon, a town famous for being the title of a popular song. The car I hired to take me there hummed for three hours, mostly past fields shorn of their crops, with barns and granaries between them.

In all our trips to auctions around Ontario, Shareef and I had never ventured as far as where I had now decided to live, sight unseen.

The last five kilometres of the trek were on a narrow dirt road. On the two or three occasions when a vehicle approached in the distance, my driver slowed, climbed his car onto the weedy hump on the side of the road, and let the other vehicle pass before accelerating again.

By the time we arrived at White Lake, it was dusk. The trees were tall and close together and, even in the fall, obscured nearly all the driveways. We knew we were passing another cottage whenever we saw nailed to a tree a homemade wooden plaque, usually illustrated, bearing a family name: THE WILLISES, with a picture of a quacking duck; THE HARVEYSONS, with a picture of two alert-looking Labradors; THE LEFEBVRES, with an etching of a cabin and evergreens.

Finally, we arrived at my destination: THE STYCKSES OF WHITE LAKE, no illustration. For a minute, I fancied myself a pioneer somewhere unknown and unfamiliar (even if that somewhere already had a plaque, and other inhabitants long before that plaque).

I got out of the car, retrieved my bags.

The cottage was perfect in its spareness. The living area was a rectangular space, orange with cedar panelling. There was a dusty cast iron stove in the middle, across from a large window overlooking a steep downward slope towards the lake. A gaunt sofa whose leather was cracked like the heel of a foot. A handmade wood shelf, a handmade wood coffee table. A knotted rug, formerly a light colour. One small bedroom, and a smaller bathroom. Some books, a deck of cards, and videotapes, not many. Everything was just short of decrepit.

I took down whatever picture frames were on the walls of the cottage, and books and tapes from the shelves, and put them all in the shed outside, next to a red plastic canoe and some life jackets. I put my own sheets on the bed.

Early in our relationship, Shareef explained to me that he felt safer when he was part of a community, or at least when he was with the objects and relics of that community. Whether it was among his friends and co-workers in the city, or in the sleepy towns with all their well-attended auctions, or in Abu Dhabi with his family, or in a land memorialized on that pre-1948 globe — he needed to feel a part of those places and their people.

After my exhibition, he said, "I can't tell you how nice it feels to be the subject of a piece of art on someone's wall. It's like I'm with them somehow, like I'm important and safe." I thought he was teasing me, but then I realized he really meant it.

What Shareef craved was what made me feel weighed down, constricted. I wanted to be away from all the people and their trappings. I felt safer in leaving.

ONCE EVERY WEEK OR TWO I had to venture out of the cottage for food. Supply trips were mostly to nearby Fenelon Falls, which had a couple of decent-sized grocers. Eileen had allowed me the use of her husband's massive pickup that was parked at the cottage when I arrived. Just ascending into that truck required me to raise one leg nearly to my waist to get a foothold, before huffing the rest of my body up into it. I may as well have been entering a spaceship.

Packages had to be picked up from the Fenelon Falls post office. It turned out this was one of the main meeting places for people from town. Everyone had ample opportunity to look me over whenever I went. Thankfully, at least the middle-aged, russet-bearded clerk behind the counter—Wayne, according to his fringed name tag—did not belabour his interactions with me.

"You're from around Toronto, I'm guessing," he said without glancing up, after I'd asked for my mail. It was my second or third time at the post office.

"Yes."

"The look and the accent gave it away."

"Ah."

"Here for a good while, then?"

"We'll see, I guess."

"You are. Nobody gets this many packages if they're not. Here you go. Have a nice day."

My packages mostly contained art supplies that I ordered. I had not anticipated running out so quickly, except that my cottage had no internet connection and poor cell reception, which Eileen had warned me about. At that time of year, there was little to do but feed the stove, and try to work. I had also ordered a number of warmer sweaters.

When I descended the steep hill to the dock on White Lake, I could see all the other cottages. They sat in a row from one end of the water to the other, each surrounded by cushions of dark greenery. If I counted the lit windows, it was never more than half. They were too far away for me to see people in them.

I painted the lake first, and then the trees. I painted the few motorboats that still braved the lake in the weather. I painted the cottages, and what I thought was in the cottages. I painted Shareef, from memory. I designated a corner of the cottage for my discarded works, which were all of them.

I was heating up the kettle for tea when a dog visited. It got up on its hind legs and peered through my window.

It was scruffy and black, with brown markings on its legs and face. It had a collar and seemed healthy, so I assumed it was a neighbour's pet, allowed to roam. I tried to ignore it. The dog left before the tea had finished steeping.

I became used to simple sounds. My tires crunching on the gravel when I arrived home from town, or chipmunks rustling through the leaves tessellated on the ground. I ate simple foods: bread, cheese, sometimes a premade dip if the Fenelon Falls grocer had a package left.

The dog became a daily visitor. Sometimes he simply lay in the back deck and snored for an hour or two, and sometimes he only looked at me for a few minutes and left. I heard him bark maybe once, at a bird that flapped off a tree branch too suddenly for his taste.

The ancientness of my surroundings appealed to me: the width of the trees, the absence of footpaths. It made me feel a part of the land, rooted there somehow. Considering I was probably newer there than anyone else for miles, it embarrassed me to catch myself feeling this way.

"Pull yourself together," I once said aloud to no one as I clomped through undergrowth on an afternoon walk.

I often went down to the lake, in gloves and a balaclava, and looked back up the hill at the cottage. I liked to do this after sunset, when it was light enough out that I could make out shadows, but dark enough that the shadows could be anything. I had hoped that North Africa's mountains would come to me in that view, but they did not. It was too cold, probably. The associations were all wrong. It felt useless to keep pretending I was home.

ON A NIGHT in the middle of December, I heard from outside my door the growl of a running motor and the crunch of gravel. Such unnatural noises were so intrusive when I wasn't the one causing them. I already had a cast iron poker in one hand from working the stove, and I took it with me to the door. My phone was in my other hand.

A tall, bulky man got out of a truck. Trucks like that were common in these parts, but men that towered over them were not. I could feel my heart thump.

I turned on the light outside my front door. The man was not wearing a uniform, but I thought I recognized who it was.

"Oh, hello there, Miss Noor," he said.

"Is that you? The guy from the post office?" I shouted. "What are you doing here?"

"Well, first of all, no need for that weapon in your hand! I come in peace, and would hate to leave in pieces," he laughed. "You'll have to excuse me for that one. Yes, it's me, Wayne from the post office."

"What are you doing here, Wayne?"

"What I'm doing is wishing you a merry Christmas, that's first of all. But another thing is that you haven't been around the post office in a while, and your packages have been piling up. I thought why not do a little favour for the new girl in town. Can't take the mailman out of me, I guess."

Wayne reached into his trunk and pulled out several boxes, brought them over, and laid them in a stack near my doorstep. I tightened my grip on the poker every time he came near.

"Well, that's about all. Do you want me to bring them inside for you?" he asked.

"No, there is good, thanks. You didn't have to come here for this."

"Oh, that I know. But it's no trouble."

"How did you know where I live? None of the packages have my address."

Wayne laughed from his belly, as if I had just told the best joke in the world. "Well, the thing is," he said, "you can't drive around in Old Man Stycks's 1991 two-toned F-150 — the one with that dent in the front fender from his run-in with a poor baby deer — and expect not to be telling on yourself." He smiled and shook his head at me.

"You knew him, I guess," I said.

"Yeah, I did a few things for the Styckses here and there. In fact I helped them get that stove you have in there off the truck and installed. Just saying that takes me back. That was when I was in my last year of high school."

Wayne looked over my shoulder inside the cottage and nearly took a step forward. Then he gave a half cough to cover up his change of mind and turned to leave.

"Listen, Miss Noor, you might think about getting out there and meeting some people. No one will bite, I assure you."

"Wayne, if you don't mind..." I began.

"In fact, tomorrow there's an auction at the Fenelon Falls community hall. We're selling off a couple of estates. One of them being my mother's, as a matter of actual fact. She passed away a few months ago. I'm trying to find new homes for all her things, because I sure don't have the room myself. Anyway, it's a good place to look around, see folks from town, that sort of thing. No obligation to buy."

MY DREAMS THAT night were of Shareef and me again, travelling together in the mountains. Wistful now, suffused with the glum calls of birds that I never heard in Algeria. Our trails were murky and unknown, like neither of us knew where we were going.

I woke up in the morning with this thought: one final auction. This one without Shareef. I would go, I would see, and I would return to the cottage, released of him.

I arrived early enough to view the lots before bidding opened at ten. Compared to some of the auction sites I'd seen, the Fenelon Falls community centre was large and looked recently constructed. It had a hockey rink attached to it, and as I passed by, I saw children in uniforms taking some steps on the shimmering ice and falling over on their faces.

The auction was held in the main hall, which was festooned with Christmas decorations. A large tree had been hauled in for the occasion, with an oversized manger scene set up underneath it. Some people gathered, coffees in hand, to admire it.

Automatically, I started walking up and down the three long rows of metal tables that were lined up end to end, giving everything the careful once-over that I had seen many times from Shareef. Twice, I asked the volunteer staff if I could touch the merchandise, and twice I was met with a warm "Of course, dear."

I had an unexpected feeling: perhaps ... I was interested in some items. There was a rocking chair made of solid oak that I could see putting next to the stove at the cottage. I could fit it in the truck easily.

It took me a long time to wade through everything.

At the end of the third and last row, I found them: three framed original oil paintings, a sign beneath them claiming they were by Norval Morrisseau. Bright as explosions.

Their lines assured, the colours unreserved. They bore his famous signature in Cree syllabics.

An auction clerk standing nearby handed me a binder with some certificates of authentication. They seemed to be inkjet printouts on ordinary paper, with no original seal, not even letterhead. If I had suspicions about provenance, the certificates would not have put them to rest.

The painting I liked most, the one I knew was coming home with me, was called *Three Giant Moose*. Two orange moose faced each other, with lumps of mountains behind them. On one of the mountains, tiny in the distance, was another moose, the third.

"It's art that makes an impact on you, no doubt," the clerk said. "Think of how beautiful it could be in your home."

I found a seat in the middle of the audience, my paddle on my lap. An older woman seated nearby was tilting a bag of roasted almonds into her mouth. She turned to me and said, "Strange time to be a tourist. You haven't gone to the falls yet, have you? Well, don't bother, they aren't much to see this time of year."

"I'm not a tourist," I said. "And I've seen the falls. Between you and me, they're nothing much to look at most times of the year, are they?" It surprised me that I felt comfortable enough to say this, in this new town, as though I was one of its own.

The woman folded up her empty almond bag. She was considering me anew.

"What are you after here?" I asked.

"I'm sorry?"

"I mean, what are you looking for in this auction?"

"Oh, right, right. I guess we'll see how it goes. I think maybe there was a credenza..."

"Yeah, I saw it too. Edwardian, if I'm not mistaken. Did you know any of the deceased?"

"One of them, a little," the woman said sheepishly.

A while after the auctioneer began trotting out lots for bidding, Wayne lumbered into the hall. He had on a black plastic cap with a red logo of a semi-trailer. A flannel shirt was baggy over his gut, and his curly beard overran his face.

When he saw me, Wayne touched a finger to his hat and drooped his lower lip but did not break stride as he looked for a seat in the back by himself. I didn't like that he might think my presence at the auction meant I was okay with his visit the night before, but I forgot about it soon enough. The woman next to me got quite talkative, which I did not mind at all.

THREE GIANT MOOSE only cost me a sliver more than the average price that one of my pieces sold for at my exhibition.

But even that relatively small amount cleared the reserve price. There was one other bidder, but, after a couple of rounds against me, he contented himself with having snapped up the other two paintings.

When the auction was over, a few people came up to congratulate me on my purchase. One of them, an older gentleman, fetched his son to help me secure the painting in the flatbed of my truck. He also found a blanket and a tarp to wrap around it for the trip home.

I hung *Three Giant Moose* in the cottage. It had an entire wall to itself.

There is no explaining the sense of completeness it gave me. The painting was probably a fake, but I was a fake, too—with my art, and especially with my perception that I belonged in these woods that weren't mine. Yet both the painting and I fit where we were. It was a feeling that made sense, but also didn't. A feeling that I didn't want to own, but was persistent.

It was better than any feeling I'd had in North Africa, or in my old basement in the city, or with anyone.

Every escape I had ever made felt correct.

The next day, even the neighbour's dog barked in glee at *Three Giant Moose* when he saw it through my front window. I did have some sausages cooking on the stove-top, also.

❦

TWO NIGHTS LATER, I was still elated by my purchase. The specific curvature and sureness of its strokes kept both startling and humbling me, making me want to learn more about the piece and the tradition and history it came from. The painting also inspired some concepts for a few works of my own, which I spent some time sketching, making copious notes.

I ate better too, and that night's dinner, a rich macaroni that I prepared myself, was especially satisfying.

I lay on the sofa to rest. The fire popped and crackled. The radio played the only music I could find on the airwaves in this area—country music—at a low volume, rustling with static.

A loud, urgent barking woke me. It was followed by the crush of gravel and sticks from outside the cottage.

Was it Wayne, coming for me uninvited and unwanted, yet again? I realized the lights were on all around me, signalling that I was inside. I would have to face him, tell him to go away. I went to the fireplace and seized the poker, the brilliant colours of the painting smearing at the edge of my vision. I pulled the window curtain to look.

It wasn't Wayne. It wasn't anyone.

All I could make out in the dark was the shadowy outline of a large animal, maybe an elk. Or a moose. I wouldn't know the difference.

The animal stepped gingerly back towards the woods, unperturbed. The neighbour's dog kept barking anyway.

Every escape I had ever made was correct.

THE REFLECTED SKY

Front door, exterior

Welcome back, Astrid. I hope you had a great time in South America. It's been a wonderful summer here, and yours has been a wonderful home. Thank you.

Coat hook on the inside of the front door

My infatuation started with a coat hook. I used this one to hold my jacket, which I wore often. I come from a warmer clime than you, so even your July and August sometimes made my bones—how do you say it—crack? Crackle? Beatrix laughs at these failings of mine. You too, go ahead, laugh away.

Kitchen counter

Some bookkeeping. Your landlord has received transfers for each of the three months I've been here, and I have records in case you need them. The electrical and water bills have been paid in full. Some of Beatrix's rowdy friends broke one of your wicker chairs, and for that I left you an appropriate amount in this envelope, so that you can replace it.

Let me say again that it was a sheer pleasure to sublet your apartment, a pleasure that could only be enhanced by meeting you, which unfortunately won't happen. My plane leaves tonight, several days before you return.

Top kitchen drawer

My compliments on the sound investment you've made: these are amazing implements. Sharp and unforgiving. Well, that pair of pigeons I cooked for Beatrix must have thought so anyway! Unfortunately, their butchering went to waste. It turns out Beatrix is a vegetarian. I recovered well enough, however. Made her a mean (meaning "good," I have learned) batch of authentic hummus, in the style of my Palestinian ancestors.

Photograph affixed to refrigerator

This photo of you is my favourite, Astrid. All the hours our mutual friend Pico and I whiled away together over heavily sugared tea in those Beirut cafés overlooking the Mediterranean, laughing and planning my summer in Toronto, and not once did he mention that you were so beautiful. A glaring omission.

And, if you'll allow me to wax a bit longer, you project a joy that seems so native to your face, smiling widely, your cheek pressed to the cheek of this unknown Asian woman. She seems to have integrated well, no? The joy seems native to her face also.

Stack of yellow sticky notes on the hallway shelf

I remember once reading in Nabokov (himself an adoptive anglophone) about an obsessive domestic annotator by the name of Dr. Goldsmith, who littered his home with little informational notes for its renters. And so by now I'm sure you have noticed what I have done in homage: on most items in your house, you will find I've pasted a yellow note (or, for my more verbose moments, two or three of them daisy-chained together). If you can decode my terrible handwriting, it might give you something to read in those first few hours back at your — forgive me — pad.

Bed

This might be a bit uncouth to say, but Beatrix and I loved your bed. Soft, yet bouncy. You know, it started out so well with her. I first spotted her at the Metro grocery.

Shoulder-length hair, her nimble fingers picking out cherries. As she moved across the aisles of produce, a vertical row of black letters on the inside of her left arm made fleeting appearances. I feel it is a sign of great self-belief to mark your body with language.

Admiring her, I remembered I had a real home base in the city, and a flush of confidence came over me. I said to myself, let's do as the natives do and accost a woman in an improbable place, showing boldness that she will no doubt recall with gratitude later. We talked about beets—yes, beets. I said I liked them because they looked so picturesquely dangerous in a salad. It was a wasted adverb, Astrid. I have almond eyes, and my manner is easy; for some, that is enough.

The next time I saw Beatrix, she wore long sleeves. Pity.

It was on your bed, when I finally pinned that girl down, that I discovered, among other things, that those letters on Beatrix's unsheathed arm spelled nothing less mundane than BE-A-TRICKS.

Living room wall

At six or seven years old, I learned my first words of English from little Peter, little Jane, and their little dog, Pat. They were the stars of a British series of children's books imported to the Middle East, chosen for its torturous pedagogy. Shortly thereafter, I made the decision that one day I would permanently abandon my mother tongue (and all the refuge countries of my youth) and join Peter, Jane, and Pat in their Western wonderland of wheat-blond hair, green lawns, and shorts. I dreamt of building a fortress for just the four of us (dogs had to be counted, as I understood it), with strong walls, where the only interlopers were the birds floating in the azure sky. My new friends and I would feel secure together, our conversations effortless and happy.

The point is that those bores of linguistic iteration made a big impression on me. I tell you this in case your next-door neighbour Janey mentions my fit of uncontrollable laughter when she knocked on my door one afternoon, bearing her sizable breasts (and some iced tea) on a platter, and invited me to join her, her boyfriend, Pete, and their roommate, Patricia, for an evening on their back deck.

Since then, I've gotten nothing but the evil eye from them.

Rack of vinyl records, living room
Your music is mostly alien to me (who are these Indigo Girls?), but our dinner guests, Beatrix's friends, enjoyed it very much. They were surprised I had such good taste, "all things considered." I took the liberty of not correcting them. By the early evening, I had in my mind given them all names like Jonathan and Jacob and Charlotte and, to

add a little flavour, Isabella. (They never introduced themselves, so what choice did I have?) They danced and sang and said to keep the drinks coming. Beatrix was gliding with happiness. I was the host, but I don't think anyone noticed when I couldn't take it anymore and left after a short while. I lingered at a bar nearby and only returned when I was sure that every last guest had slunk out.

I did notice you have a Cat Stevens compilation. That bird flew in exactly the wrong direction, didn't he?

Canvas map of the world, hallway

Aren't you astonished when you meet someone these days and the subject of travel comes up? They've always visited so many countries, and they keep such precise mathematics about it (for example, our mutual friend Pico claims a stunning forty-nine conquests to his name). By contrast, Astrid, I see that your own number is quite pedestrian, if the push-pins on this map are up to date. Your current jaunt to South America will mark only your fourth international trip. With such a slender figure, how can you look your friends in their wanderlust-frenzied eyes?

On the topic of Pico, I understand that, despite recommending that I sublet your apartment, he's never actually been here? Well, I told him to look for the copper-bricked, ivy-swathed, three-storey house on Howland. I said he can stroll right through the front door, as it is always open. (No fortress here.) There will be a stairwell leading to three units: ground floor (Janey's), second floor (Astrid's/mine), and third floor (vacant). Come anytime, I said, whenever all your journalism dies down. I went as far as saying I missed seeing him.

Look, I know about the vortex of a busy career. After all, I met Pico because of work. Did he tell you that? Looking for someone who could decipher Arabic for a story he was working on, he answered one of my ads about translation. He asked, somewhat oddly, where I lived. I guess journalists can be very direct about such things? After some hesitation, I said Beirut. Immediately he exulted, sending several emojis. He told me he had planned a trip to Lebanon that very summer, and would I be interested in meeting up once he was there? Soon, we were traipsing through the dingy, pulsating streets of Hamra, enjoying the coffee (and the immaculately nosed barista) at the Café Younes, and clapping and twisting our arms to the chaabi music at Metro al Madina. I even bargained down a cab driver for Pico before his day trip to the ruins of Byblos, the one whose stunning photos you must have liked on his various social accounts. (As a personal victory for me, the entire time, Pico did not make any remarks on my English skills.)

One late night, as we sat drinking in one of those squalid bars on Mar Mikhael, Pico told me I *needed* to visit Toronto. "Next summer," he said, "and I am not asking." He proceeded to give me all the reasons, the way only someone can whose love for his hometown is deep and unshakable. It sounded truly unmissable.

I guess I am still waiting to be ushered into the summertime idyll Pico promised me in this city, full of vibrant patios, barbecues, and, most importantly, warm friends like you, Astrid. Instead, today, for example, after waiting two days for an answer to a casual hello message, I received this from Pico: *Sorry, bud. The trouble is, I'm not as free to hang out here as when I'm on vacation.*

Living room window overlooking Howland Avenue
Beatrix is consumed with being outside, outside, outside. Let's go to Christie Pits Park and watch a film under the stars! Let's go for ice cream and roam Ossington Street, laughing and dribbling on our shirts! Let's hit the waterfront, let's crash a farmers' market, let's die of happiness!

For the life of her, Beatrix cannot understand why a tourist would want to stay in the apartment as much as I do.

Photograph on the bulletin board
This must be around the third grade? Or fourth? It took me a while, but I think I found you, Astrid, on the far right of

the photo, seated, big-cheeked like a canary. As it happens, I had my own fifth-grade class picture handy (what a thing to lug with me on vacation, I'm sure you're thinking). Little me is also seated and, fortuitously, on the far left. I could not resist lining the two pictures up together to make one big class, half pale and half tawny. Our shoulders are touching!

Backside of the hallway shelf

Okay, it wasn't just that oddball Dr. Goldsmith who did it. From the first time I stepped into this house, I couldn't help but notice that you and your downstairs neighbour Janey had developed a running repartee by way of the sticky notes in the stairwell. A mix of hellos, thank-yous, reminders, requests, jokes, niceties, expressions of friendship, haikus, and other prattle. Lovingly handwritten, all. The entire wall was covered in scribbled-up yellow. This is what they call an "inside" joke, as I understand? (Though, I note, it is on the *outside* of your homes.) The pair of you created a shared code and were busy using it to write your world away.

I guess I thought: Why not add a third cent to your two?

On the spine of the copy of Wuthering Heights
on the bookshelf

One of your notes to Janey has stayed with me. I make sure
to peek at it every time I climb the stairs:

> J.,
>   *Is this love?*
>   *It is it is.*
>   *(Us, in a parenthesis.)*
>   A.

How sweet to feel so near to someone and to, also,
actually be near them.

Today, after reading this note yet again, I kept turning
its words in my mouth so much that I carried on going
right up the stairs, past your apartment number 2, and
right to apartment number 3 (vacant). You make me forget
myself, Astrid.

Bedroom light switch

I keep discovering the fissures in myself, in this construction,
over and over. At fifteen, I asked an American exchange
student at my school in Beirut if he would like to use my
"rubber," and he guffawed so violently he almost choked
on his gum. At twenty-five, a research supervisor left an
angry red circle around the phrase "this data" in one of my

reports. Tonight, before bedtime, I said "close the lights, please," only to receive from Beatrix, of all people (*Beatrix!*), an amused, confident correction in response. Why does this keep happening? What more is there? When will my command be impregnable?

Folded white panties on the bedside table

Yours. You did a good job scrubbing the place clean of all your clothes, but these stragglers were hiding behind the bathroom hamper. Unfortunately, they caused me a bit of trouble when Beatrix found them. Shaking with disgust, she nudged them towards me with the very tip of her big toe. I will spare you the details, except to say that at one point during the mess that ensued, as Beatrix was swearing up and down never to let me touch her again, I tried a line I'd been saving for quite some time:

"Quoth the raven-haired beauty, 'Nevermore'?"

I'd been hanging on to that one ever since I was a teen-ager still learning English, voraciously catching up on American children's poems. I don't know how many hours I spent turning it over in my head, admiring its casual, thrown-away knowledge, smoothing it to perfection. Now admittedly, Beatrix was not the ideal target (chestnut hair, rather illiterate), but still, I expected back more than: "Huh? What are you . . . you know what? I don't even care. Just don't contact me."

Astrid, I am increasingly disappointed with my visit. Nothing of me has landed as I wanted it to.

Bedside drawer

Incidentally, you and Beatrix wear the same size. I was able to ascertain this only because, when she's sleeping, Beatrix becomes completely, totally insensate.

Mother-of-pearl side table, living room

Beatrix is here every day now. Her disavowal of me didn't take, I guess. Sincerely, I struggle to understand how she managed to spend her nights before she found me. The only relief is that she is a late riser, so at least she has ceded mornings to me.

Well, I cede my mornings to you. I am awed by you, Astrid. As I sit in this living room, it strikes me how all the world has come to you. Look at your mid-century buffet, Danish, the teak wood ribbed with the rays fleeing in through the window slats. Look at your antique rug, once Persian, since stripped and re-dyed, soft against my feet. Look at your heavy hexagonal coffee table, nemesis to many of my toes, a Moorish mosaic. Look at your green sari (a costume you wore to an Indian wedding, I assume), now covering half a window and flecking the room with its sparkle. Look at your record player, classically American. Look at this colourful throw on your sofa, maybe Peruvian alpaca or some such. And look, finally, at this Levantine side table of yours, graciously draped with a piece of Palestinian embroidery.

How easily you have absorbed all these elements. How effortlessly have they been deracinated and made to thrive again on your sovereign territory.

Keys on the living room coffee table

When I visualized my summer here in your apartment, I may have allowed myself to envision a suitable fling for some of the duration. I thought maybe someone bright, droll, mostly braless under her tank tops. The sheer foolish hubris of such thinking occurred to me as we were standing in the stairwell, Beatrix and I, our sword-clang conversation finally nearing the usual climax: Beatrix slicing into me at full volume about something or other (if memory serves, this time I was guilty of not appreciating her friends).

"Does this have to happen in the stairwell?" I asked.

"Does your cruelty have to happen in my *life!*" she retorted, slamming her hand against the wall.

A couple of yellow notes fluttered down. Hearing the commotion, Janey burst out of her door. She asked if everything was all right, and Beatrix, without any shame, crumpled into her. Janey put her arm around Beatrix and caressed the fleshy bottom of her shoulder.

(Total strangers, and in an instant, they understood each other so well they pressed their skins against one another, as if they were kin.)

In short, in Beatrix, I got a dramatic, humourless, chore of a human being, whose admitted bralessness has long since lost all appeal. I wish I could erase her (with my rubber?) from this vacation. Worst of all, whenever I think I have finally driven her away, she comes back as if nothing happened. A fling that refuses to be flung.

Speaking of driving, I purchased a car early in my Canadian stay. It's parked in front of the house, the old silver Honda. I've left you the keys and transferred the ownership to your name. Please enjoy.

Bathroom mirror

As a boy, I played peekaboo with mirrors — testing them. I would move out of the mirror's view, and then dart back in as fast as I could, to see if it would still show my reflection or, caught off guard, accidentally show me someone else. Someone more interesting, better. (Perhaps my little friends Peter and Jane?) Silly, yes. I was a child, conducting experiments on his world.

In your apartment I have been playing this game again, with this mirror. This mirror, which has seen you in the milk of your nudity how many times? If I zipped into this mirror's view before it understood what was happening, maybe I could glimpse you in it. Maybe the mirror would be tired, or asleep, or unaware, and, instead of trying to reflect my alien image, would feed me the image it has seen countless times, an easy image, an image of you.

Unfortunately, the best I could see was the reflected sky, streaming in through the windowpane.

Amaryllis pot in the living room

Janey has a key? You did not tell me this, Astrid. Today, as I was coming home from a trip to your Royal Ontario Museum (keeping a running tally of pilfered artifacts the whole time, naturally), I found her quietly pulling my door shut. She said she had been making sure the plants were okay, on your instructions. She said it almost to herself, as if she owed me no excuse for the invasion.

I suppose *plants* warrant a check-in every now and then.

Underside of the writing table

Beatrix, that bitch. She got it in her head that these are "love letters" that I am writing. So now I have a waste-basket full of yellow shreds, strewn like plucked feathers.

Don't worry, Astrid. I will write them again for you.

Leather-bound notebook on bottom shelf

I think you forgot to take this with you, or otherwise hide it better, and for that I am very grateful. There was a passage where you delicately described that time you and your friend Mary-Anne were on your bed, and you were both weeping over some deeply tragic event in your life (I can't remember what, I was very sleepy by that point), and suddenly, unexpectedly, there were your lips, and there were Mary-Anne's, and there were rivulets of tears flowing between you two and... it just happened!

You are generally a good writer, Astrid, but you were masterful on that page. Your words, even the misspellings and the lapses in grammar, felt as real as the thick walls within which they were born. Even if it was merely a description of a heartfelt first kiss, my admiration for you grew infinitely. (Between the two of us, the first time I read it, my admiration was so great it required nearly no tactile inducement for it to tumble out all over your hardwood floor.)

I know you will probably not like this, but I ripped that page out of your journal. A memento of this secret you have inadvertently let me wrest from you.

I keep it with me at all times now, close to my heart.

Under the sofa

I have not been able to tell Beatrix that I am leaving soon. The prospect of whatever meltdown will take place when I do is more than I want to deal with. A woman like her is unaccustomed to not having her way. At least she has plenty of distractions. Do you know that she has her whole "gang" over here most every day now? They still don't talk to me much, except to tell me how they just *cannot live* without my hummus.

You know who else loves the hummus? Janey! She and Beatrix are suddenly good friends. When I am sitting near the veranda, stealing covert looks at Janey's backyard down below, I can sometimes see Beatrix sitting with Janey and her boyfriend under that patio umbrella, tousling their dog's head and laughing uproariously. She is content with them.

After one such afternoon the other day, the two of them climbed back upstairs, and, thinking I was out of the house, Janey used her key to let Beatrix back in. Without bothering to knock first.

This place is no longer mine, Astrid. I am only here to put chickpeas in your food processor.

Bottom railing of the veranda door

Is that Pico I just saw? Lounging like a reptile on Janey's deck? While I crouch here on surreptitious lookout, afraid of being detected?

The last message I received from him—another apology—was over a month ago.

Inside the metal bedpost

I finally informed Beatrix that I'm leaving in a few days. After an interlude of protests and recriminations, she promised to stay with me for all my remaining time here, get my address in Beirut, and visit often in an effort to try to keep us "together" long distance. Her words: "I will *will* us to stay together if I have to."

You can see how that was too much for me. I found a flight out of the city tonight.

I guess this is goodbye.

I've done my best to leave your place in as good a state as I found it. I tidied and dusted, as much as I could in the short time I had. I cleaned the fridge and stove. I checked that I hadn't left anything of myself behind. I ran to the vacant upstairs unit (yes, all right, I used to live there before subletting your place) to pick up all my remaining belongings (yes, all right, I had lived there for many years). I won't be needing them here anymore.

I'll head to Beirut first, see if I can make it mine. The rolling blackouts might get tiresome, not to mention the political upheavals. If Beirut doesn't work out, well, I guess there's Egypt. Or maybe the Emirates. I don't know.

If you're wondering, yes, I recognize that, in that first conversation I had with Pico, when he asked where I lived, I should have just said Toronto, plainly and truthfully. I am embarrassed that I did not. But I thought he posed the question because he detected some foreignness in me, in how I spoke or acted. As an instinctive defence, I said Beirut, even though I had not lived there since I was a child. (It turned out that he only wanted to know what my address was to include it on our contract for translation services.)

I did not panic when I saw how jubilant Pico was at the prospect of us meeting. A work or family obligation can always be invented as an excuse to be unavailable (as Pico himself has capably demonstrated). But then I thought: What's stopping me from meeting him in Beirut? It's a lovely city, with charm and history. Maybe I could have a vacation, too.

Once there, it was so easy for Pico to see me as a native. My face was swarthy, my beard dark. The Arabic I spoke to the locals was creaky with disuse, but how could a delirious Canadian traveller tell the difference?

We, genuinely, had the best time.

That Pico recommended I sublet your apartment for my "visit" to Toronto, an apartment in my own building—that was, it seems, purely a coincidence (though I suppose it was not so unlikely: I'd mostly pasted my flyers close to home). Several times, I wondered whether Pico had somehow divined my secret, whether this was his way of telling me it was okay, of "bringing me in," as they say. The more I talked to him, however, the more it became clear this was not the case. I had somehow befriended the friend of my neighbour.

The prospect of "vacationing" in my own building was a strange one, but I considered it. I thought of you. I had seen you flitting in and out of the apartment before, amber hair floating softly behind you, adding little notes to your stairwell every day.

We've never spoken. In all the time we lived one floor apart, I don't think you ever passed your beautiful eyes over me. You never saw me.

Apologies for leaving on this abrupt note, but I have to hurry.

All my best to you, Astrid. My love, too.

Front door, exterior

Astrid!

You're back today right?! WB! I need to know everything about Chile.

FYI, heard loud slamming coming from your place last night. Came up and balcony door was wide open, crazy wind blowing in. Your African light thingy fell and cracked, and there was a big mess of yellow paper everywhere — from that guy you rented to? (NOT our kind of ppl, but that's another story.) I cleaned up as much as possible. A pile of crap is the last thing you need on your first day home.

Come have some iced tea this week! I want you to meet my new friend Bea.

Jane xx

ENJOY YOUR LIFE, CAPO

What you have to do is silence the world. You have to tell the world to quit wailing, to calm itself, to let you think. Just as important: you have to pick *one* world, and listen only to that world's wailing, that world's screams. Nothing else. Otherwise, you will be like all the ashen crazies tramping down the street, cursing their imagined enemies while their minds, like their clothes and lives, disintegrate into nothing.

Romero tells me this. He is focused, goal-oriented. He has kept us on track even when I have become unreliable. Our operation is almost complete. It is papered, and not illegal, and none of us will go to prison for it. If I repeat these facts enough, they might even matter.

Why can't you enjoy your life, capo? This is Romero's terminology, not mine. He is used to making real money, so criminality does not perturb him. Bridle Path mansions are in our future, he says, and infinity pools, and opportunities to supplement our wives.

I don't really want all that. What I want most is silence. Since the tumult started, since children began to be unearthed from the rubble of downed buildings, I ache for silence. It is one thing for my wife, Marcy, and my daughter, Firdaos, to be glued to their Twitter accounts and their satellite stations—finding more reasons to wail, more seeds for their future nightmares—but I cannot do that. I am trying to work.

Self-preservation is crucial. When I realized things were becoming overwhelming, I asked Firdaos to show me how to mute words on my phone. During May 2021, the major ones are obvious: Palestine, Israel, Jerusalem, Gaza, Sheikh Jarrah. But the seepage was persistent. Soon, I had to mute the names of tiny villages and neighbourhoods, the names of the ones who were killed, the names of the arrestees and detainees, the home defenders, the worshippers, the healers, the reporters, the hunger strikers, the passersby, the children, the babies—one by one, as soon as I found out that they, too, had become part of that distant, deafening inferno.

The amount we have been promised is immense. It takes my breath away, to put it in romantic terms. But in exchange for this amount, our co-conspirators want our technology immediately.

Yesterday, if possible, in light of the current situation, says Romero.

And so we have been meeting them by video conference all day for the past three days, with scant regard for our differing time zones, trying to finish the paperwork. As we do, I have been learning to suppress my hatred. You work on that sort of thing gradually. You focus on the areas of overlap in your lives, not the areas of — what's the diplomatic term? — conflict. The strategy works. With each meeting, we grow a little closer, feigning connection on the basis of little human facts about each other. *You, too, have children? You, too, experience sun, rain, relatives, death?* A measured exchange to make ourselves mutually acceptable. Within these bounds, we appear to enjoy one another.

Then our work becomes a transaction, and nothing more. I force myself to believe that to be true.

Is it our fault the market is stupid, capo?

Romero is right. The market works in mysterious ways. We have the buyer that we have.

Romero turns on our side chat. *Mind your body language,* he says. *You look bewildered.* I put my head on straight. My code is clean. It is without sins. Let's remember that. There can be no debate that I created it to help people. I used to fantasize about the newspaper headlines. "Local Entrepreneur Leads by Caring," or something comfortingly banal and affirming like that. A classic feel-good story. A quote from Marcy saying how proud she is of me. Perhaps a lede with one of the many patients I helped survive. And—dare I dream?—even a word or two from the original inspiration for it all, my tenacious fighter, Firdaos.

This is the world I want to belong to. But it is not the world I am in.

A TRIP TO the hospital is rarely an inspiring occasion, except that it was for me. More than two years ago now, Firdaos, then fifteen years old, was admitted for monitoring, struggling with another one of her periodic infections. By my count her fourth time, the cystic fibrosis now a familiar, unwanted guest, forcing us to grit our teeth and bear its visits until it deigns to leave. The usual cords of medical bondage were again attached to my daughter, a nurse or doctor coming in every ten minutes to check on her pulmonary function and respiratory rate.

Marcy had gotten better at putting on a brave face, but I knew she was roiling with anxiety inside. I was too. I tried to focus on prayer, but my mind kept taking refuge in logistics. All I could think was: *Can't this be done better somehow?*

A few days later, Firdaos's infection had subsided, and she was released from the hospital, a nebulizer over her face. Our whole house exhaled with her return. Not long after, I read online about new research claiming there was evidence that each human being has a unique breathing pattern. That was the kindling.

I started working up some ideas, stitching together parts of an algorithm. I couldn't afford to pay anyone to help me — by this point in my blundering, we had to check our bank account before ordering pizza — so I did all the coding myself. It took seven months before I had anything resembling a prototype.

It was buggy, and regularly timed out. That's where Romero came in. He had consulted on a few projects at DataHat, my old company. He never failed to isolate the critical issue and resolve it efficiently — a savant of software and, having seen some of his invoices, paid like one.

At my invite, he rolled up to the house on his motorbike, spitting out his toothpick on my lawn as he advanced to the front door. Sat at my desk and squinted at my monitor. Scrolled down the screen quickly, like a hyena bounding over the savannah. After complimenting my code — "clean like my mother's kitchen floor" — he tipped the chair into a reclining position and studied me.

"Salah, my friend," he said, "video intake is your issue. I can fix it. Watch the error rate vanish once I'm done."

I asked him how much. He took my right hand and told me to spread it open. "You keep four fingers, I take one," he said, tugging on my pinky. "Minority partner. You the capo, me the soldier."

From the beginning, Romero enjoyed acting like we were in the Mafia. A fun charade for two middle-aged computer programmers.

That night, I tacked on two rakat after my last salat. Then I asked Allah for guidance: he said go ahead with Romero. By then I was up to at least three or four out of the five prayers daily; my religion was back on the upswing ever since Firdaos had gotten sick.

It took Romero just three weeks to work his magic. Then we were off to the races. We consulted lawyers, applied for regulatory approvals, even commissioned some branding. Soon we were shopping around Version 1.0. My friend Husam in medical marketing introduced me to purchasing managers at local hospitals. I prepared a spiel and sang it like a lyric:

The revolutionary BreathCatch technology and API allows for the wireless monitoring of a patient's breathing and vitals. It analyzes recorded and live video (at frame rates that are within the capabilities of most phone cameras) to detect the unique "breath fingerprint" of a patient: consistent patterns in their facial features, cadence, and spatial environment as they inhale and exhale. The BreathCatch technology uses the breath fingerprint, and any deviations from it, to generate metrics about the patient's health over time.

Months of meeting after meeting, in claustrophobic Zoom rooms, sharing our screens, presenting our wares. Right at the start of the pandemic. Romero always by my side, hyping up everything I said like a human set of cymbals.

Uniformly positive feedback, I told Marcy. She had been through too much with me already. I think of the decade I spent at DataHat, complaining to her every night about the manager who co-opted all my best ideas, and made sure I never got promoted. Or the day I abruptly quit DataHat without a warning, either to the company or to Marcy. My parents had recently died, one after another in the span of a year, and the bereft child in me was acting up. I told Marcy that I needed the freedom to do things how I wanted, to not be beholden to anyone.

"Everyone in software takes a plunge like this at some point," I said.

Marcy touched my wrist. "Go for it," she said. We had some savings back then, but she still picked up tutoring sessions on the weekends to pad her teaching salary.

"I promise you won't have to do that for long," I had said.

Except that, after a couple of years of the entrepreneur's life, and with several failures under my belt, I was no longer sure that was true. Marcy had long ago stopped asking follow-up questions when I told her about a new venture, though I didn't stop volunteering answers.

"No bites yet on BreathCatch, Marcy, but lots of promising nibbles. Don't worry, this isn't like my other projects. This time the concept is innovative, solves a real problem. Romero says the feedback we've been getting means it's a matter of when, not if. You have to give people time and space for an idea to take hold in their minds."

"I believe in you, Salah," Marcy always said.

I HAVE TO FOCUS. In our side chat, Romero predicts that our co-conspirators will next want to discuss the mechanics of the escrow. What? Why? I steel myself for battle. I am so ready to put these people back in their rightful place as my foes. They are bureaucrats and government lawyers and data scientists, but from the beginning, I have had to work hard to not envision them in army fatigues. Whenever they make a demand—an "ask," is the genteel way us co-conspirators put it—it's like the hot mouth of a Tavor is pointed at my face.

But there are no Tavors in the face of a muta'awin, are there? The villas of collaborators like me are raided very infrequently, the hand restraints placed very gently on their wrists, just for show, if at all. Their dossiers are kept in an entirely separate department of Shin Bet.

Collaborator. Not a scent of treachery in that word in English. On the contrary. Before I went out on my own, did not every resumé I ever submitted to an employer describe me as "collaborative"? Collaboration is critical to creating value. And now that I have created the biggest item of value in my life, am I to suddenly stop being collaborative?

Yes, I should stop. All the time, all I want is to stop.

The second-in-command unmutes himself to relay the latest ask: "We want a window of time to inspect the software in escrow, to verify all the goods are as they should be, before we release the payment to you. Don't worry, we only need a very limited period, not nearly long enough for us to copy it all for free." (Hearty laughs from all the faces tiled on my screen.)

I waffle. Every decision is an opportunity to escape. There have been many review meetings, phalanxes of their experts inspecting the software as if it were the body of a newborn. I have held my co-conspirators' hands as they waltzed through the lines of my code, sometimes reading them aloud to each other with symphonic appreciation. Where they didn't understand something, I was the model of patience as I explained it to them, stifling every outward sign of disdain. Why, then, the need for more inspection time, when the baby is already caged in escrow, waiting to be handed to its new parents?

Romero consents on our behalf, adds a condition or two.

Every little thing does not have to be an agonizing decision, capo.

Soon, this will all be over, tossed into a dark basement of my memory and shrouded in binding confidentiality provisions. Lupara bianca, in the parlance. Then, Romero assures me, we will have nothing but comforts.

After how hard our road was, capo? You can never convince me we don't deserve it.

ROMERO AND I followed up with each purchasing manager we met, three or four times at least. Gradually, the responses evolved from "Not right now, but we'll contact you if anything changes" to "Please stop calling us, our decision is final."

We kept working, undaunted. Our clinical trials yielded good results but needed something anecdotal to tug on hearts. We knew the optimal specimen was Firdaos. Young, vibrant, and in a never-ending fight just to keep breathing—who wouldn't sympathize with that?

My relationship with my daughter then was not at its peak, not anymore. That magical time was a few years ago, when she was in middle school. Back then, my late-night coding sessions often stretched until the muezzin app on my phone signalled the time for dawn prayer. Firdaos, already showing signs of being my opposite, was an early riser.

Unbidden, she would slip out of bed and find me in the master bathroom. We would do our wudu together at the double vanity, as quietly as we could lest we disturb her mother's sleep. We'd polish off the brace of rakat, chat a while on our prayer rugs, and then move to my office. There I would show her some coding basics, watching her eyebrows rumple in concentration as she absorbed another if-else statement. When I got sleepy, she'd pester me to leave her with a coding exercise to do on her own, so she could show off how well she'd completed it the minute I opened my eyes again.

As she got older, Firdaos lost interest in coding, replacing it with reading, blog writing, Twitter debates. Her disease took a toll, too: she became more distant after every debilitating flare-up, as if she wanted to prove to her parents that she could manage on her own. My bond with her endured, but it felt mostly historical, like it wasn't based on anything current anymore. Still, sometimes if I got out of bed early enough, I might find her sitting in my office, tapping on her laptop or leafing through the newspaper. It made me happy to think of it as a sign of her lingering attachment to me.

My office was where I found Firdaos the morning that I told her about BreathCatch. She was touched that I invented a whole system to monitor her health. But the teenager in her bristled when I asked if I could install an old phone in a corner of her room.

"Don't worry," I said. "I can't see your picture. It just analyzes your breathing and sends me the information. You'll forget it's even there."

The readings arrived at my console whenever Firdaos was in camera range. If they showed that her vitals had taken a turn for the worse, I texted to ask how she was doing.

I can't believe you can figure out I'm not right from a phone cam, she texted me back once. *I haven't even coughed! It's a little creepy.*

Romero and I drafted reports based on the clinical trials, and on Firdaos. In block quotes, we said that BreathCatch showed a 97.5% accuracy rate in detecting moments when a patient's breathing was in or near distress. For software that could run off a phone cam, this seemed extraordinary to us.

Not that our precious case study was available much in those days. During the spring of 2020, the pandemic forced Firdaos's public school to shift to virtual learning, but she was so involved with all the protests going on at the time that I hardly saw her. I did see her traces, though. There were markers and large pieces of cardboard left on the living room floor, along with splayed pairs of scissors that blended hazardously into the rug. There were attempts at catchy slogans scribbled and crossed out next to aborted sketches of George Floyd. A Black girl named Adie began to frequent our backyard, she and Firdaos chatting with their masks tucked uselessly under their chins.

"I think it's good that our teenager is so engaged in the world," said Marcy. "She's not letting her condition stop her from living her life."

It was true. The movement for racial justice seemed to ignite Firdaos. She went to all the demonstrations and rallies, no longer embarrassed to be seen using her medical accoutrements if she needed them. She wrote letters to the editors of local newspapers calling out their coverage of the riots in the United States. She covered our lawn with signs bearing the names of recent victims of police violence. She even started a group called Palestinians for Ending Anti-Black Racism, through which she started organizing online.

One day I noticed that she had changed her Discord profile picture to an old photo of a full-cheeked Black woman wearing a polka-dotted bandana.

Is that an old Black Panther or something? I texted.

Wow, the ignorance, she replied.

According to the lecture my daughter later delivered, the picture was of Fatima Bernawi, one of the first Palestinian women freedom fighters. Bernawi, a Jerusalemite of Nigerian descent, had been imprisoned for attempting to

bomb an Israeli cinema in her hometown shortly after the
war in 1967. Bernawi looked like a punk rock star: angry
eyes, tongue out in defiance, jet bangs peeking out from
under her headwrap.

"I'm surprised you don't know her," Firdaos said. "You
call yourself a Palestinian?"

There's no greater accountability than that which your
children demand of you.

As the lockdown wore on through the summer, Firdaos
increasingly brought Adie inside our house for the comfort
of air conditioning, and they spent hours together in
Firdaos's room. This was against the rules at the time, but
Marcy let it slide. She said she didn't want to regulate our
daughter's life too much, not when the disease was already
in charge of most of it.

"Plus, they're both wearing their masks, aren't they?"
she added.

At first, Adie's presence in Firdaos's room tripped up
my software. So I cobbled together a patch that enabled
BreathCatch to distinguish multiple people and record
their vitals separately. It surprised me that the girls' masks
didn't degrade the quality of the readings much. With small
modifications, the software was able to detect a person's
breathing patterns no matter what they had on their face.

Those were strange times. The software had become
quite powerful, but the pandemic made it so hospital and

clinic budgets were maxed out attending to more immediate needs. I was always either distracted or in a bad mood. I started waiting until Marcy was sound asleep before coming to bed myself, just to avoid telling her how grim things looked for my new venture.

On a particularly bad day in the middle of June, I was in my car, trying to distract myself with a drive on the 401. I put on Abdul-Basit's recitation of Al-Rahman, one of my favourite suras, which I hoped would calm me. His voice as he enumerated God's blessings brought me back to the day when Marcy and I had our nikah in a small ceremony at my parents' house, and my mother played this melodic sura. Even before that day, Marcy was like the daughter my mother never had.

Marcy's family had been our next-door neighbours, and after her own mother passed away prematurely from cancer, her overwhelmed father was only too glad for preteen Marcy to spend some after-school time with the kindly, veiled immigrant lady next door. Marcy became a fixture at our house, teaching my mother some slang and explaining to her the workings of middle school; in exchange, my mother let Marcy watch her as she tended the garden or wrapped grape leaves for dinner. By the time I had completed university, I was struck by how attractive and mature Marcy had become, and how much a part of our family she already was. Marcy seemed to see something in me, too, though I don't doubt that, at least partly, she saw my mother.

It was an hour lost in this memory, and in Abdul-Basit's voice, before I even looked at my phone again and noticed a spate of missed calls from Marcy.

Firdaos's principal had called. Firdaos and Adie had been caught on closed-circuit cameras brazenly defacing school property. With black spray paint, they had scrawled RACISM HAPPENS HERE TOO on the school's front doors, across several classroom windows, and on the tennis court. They did it in broad daylight, without hoodies or hats or anything to conceal their identities. They didn't even hasten their steps as they were leaving.

The next day, Marcy and I had a video call with the principal, Ms. Warner. She was in her late fifties, with a silver bun on top of her head and a manner of speaking that made you feel she was disappointed you didn't know better. Ms. Warner wanted us to know that the school had been very sensitive to the emotions of students during this difficult time in race relations. There had been special video listening sessions that were made available, with school administrators and child psychologists present. There had been resources created for those affected, and for their allies like Firdaos. The school had even issued a formal statement in support of Black Lives Matter, which was unprecedented and, some would say, controversial.

Ultimately, however, the actions of Firdaos and Adie were unacceptable. The upshot, as I understood from reading between the lines, was that while the school would've liked to discipline the girls, they were afraid to in light of shifting public sentiment. And so they were willing to resolve the issue quietly, provided the parents of the two well-meaning (but culpable) teens paid to repair the damage.

This seemed like a reasonable solution to me, but I wanted to consult with Firdaos. I asked Ms. Warner if she had spoken to Adie's parents. Ms. Warner said that she had; the Taysons wanted time to think the matter over.

I looked at Marcy, who nodded at me to respond. "In that case," I said, "we will do the same."

ON THE SCREEN SHARE, the row marked "Escrow" is now green, meaning completed. Only a few more rows of collaboration to go.

The second-in-command mentions that he would like to revisit the intellectual property terms. I can almost hear my heart rate quickening. *Stay calm, stay calm. This is a normal business negotiation between human beings.* To prove this to myself, I go over the human traits that I have learned about the second-in-command: three children, a second wife, likes sports, does not like hot weather. That last bit I gleaned today. As part of our compulsory five minutes of small talk, the second-in-command said: "Our weather is sometimes difficult in the summer, even if we are right next to the sea."

The thing to avoid here, if I were to anticipate Romero's advice, is lingering on the words *our weather*. When the second-in-command says that, it is obviously not meant to insult, obviously not meant to inflame. I have to be very firm with myself about this. We cannot be adolescents here, trying to detect hurts where there is only normal communication. The second-in-command does not mean that he owns the weather. He simply lives in an area, and the weather in that area is, as a figure of speech, *his weather*.

The second-in-command mentioned the name of his city in our earliest introductions. A hub city for technology in their technology-proud country. It was called something ending in -*na*, I believe. Or maybe something ending in -*ya*, or -*on*. I don't remember. I made sure to expel it from my mind as soon as I heard it, so I would not be tempted to locate it on a map later. If I did look on a map, the area might seem familiar. It might have a former name that did not end in -*na* or -*ya* or -*on*, a former name in my own language, not theirs, and so one that I could not so easily forget. Perhaps his weather would be revealed to be my grandfather's old weather, or my grandmother's old weather. Perhaps I would be tempted to think of it as *my rightful weather*.

And all that for what, a figure of speech?

Let's focus. I message Romero: *I would like to keep an open mind here, but what more could they possibly want?* We are already selling them our entire technology, totally and completely.

The second-in-command says, "We would like to add that you will give us everything you may invent in the future that is in any way related to this software, or related to breathing generally."

Fury.

Is what I am hearing real? They want to lay claim not just to the best idea I have ever had but also to any ideas I may ever have? Is this what passes for a joke among them, their way of toying with the Arab they have on a string? My daughter struggles to breathe, I witness her languishing every day — yet I am to stop myself from thinking of ways to help her, or else risk losing them to these criminals?

The thought of Firdaos makes me desperate. Without warning, I turn off my computer camera and pick up my phone. I see she's changed her profile picture again — it's back to the Bernawi photo, which she hasn't used since last summer's George Floyd protests. And she's added some of my muted words in hashtags on top of it.

#FreePalestine #SaveSheikhJarrah #EndtheOccupation #EndIsraeliGenocide

Romero messages me in our side chat. *Where are you? Did you walk out? This ask is not strange, and our lawyer agrees.*

They just want to make sure you're not holding back anything. It's baked into the price.

I turn my camera back on. Borrowing some boldness from my daughter, I address the second-in-command. "So, about this request then . . . What if we say no?"

"That would be a problem," he says.

"In that case, we have a problem."

WE GOT TO KNOW the Taysons well after the graffiti incident. Adie was their only child, same as Firdaos. Their subdivision was indistinguishable from ours, medium-sized family homes with economical upgrades. They were reasonable people, amiable, but also principled.

"I'll be very honest with you, Salah," said Leonard Tayson on the phone. "I don't care to think of what Adie and Firdaos did as wrong. I think the reaction to injustice should never be what gets punished."

"What are you saying?" I asked.

"I am saying that I don't see why I would pay a single penny to that school. If they had their house in order, our girls wouldn't have felt the need to act out."

I was intrigued by this line of thinking. The chance to show solidarity with my daughter and her friend was attractive enough, especially since I was supportive of the cause. More pressing was that the school had estimated the costs of fixing the damage to be in the thousands of dollars, and that kind of cash was always going to be tough to hand over.

In the end, we and the Taysons sent a joint letter to Ms. Warner not only declining her proposal but instead providing a list of demands (authored mostly by Leonard and his wife, Simone) for changes that the school should make with a view to fostering racial equity and awareness.

The girls were elated. For a while, Firdaos switched her profile picture to a photo of me, her, and Marcy posing as a slightly sunburned family on a trip to Mexico a few years back. *My crew, my pride*, she had written underneath it. She also made a point of emerging from her usual self-imposed confinement in her bedroom to cheerfully interact with Marcy and me every couple of hours.

As the news trickled out, us parents began to enjoy the status of quasi-celebrities in our neighbourhood. Clusters of girls and boys from Firdaos's school showed up in our backyard, nodding vigorously and raising their fists when they saw Marcy or me appear in the window.

"The funniest part," Firdaos said, "is that kids from school have been stealing my Bernawi picture and using it for their own profiles. She's like our Black power mascot now."

"Did you tell them who Bernawi is?" I asked. I am always slightly incredulous when I hear of people showing sympathy to Palestinians. My instinct is to wonder if they understand the danger their support poses to them.

"I told them the truth: that she's an old freedom fighter, an absolute icon."

I admired Firdaos's nerve. It was a trait that, if I'd ever had it, had been wrung out of me long ago. When I was around her age and new to Canada, the teacher in my high school English class asked me where I was from. I was naive then and blurted the word "Palestine," the name of the place my parents were born and taught me I was from. The class rustled as it sensed a disturbance in the air, and the teacher murmured, "Interesting, interesting," before swiftly moving on. Soon after, the school newspaper, usually a peppy affair rife with picture-heavy updates about the latest Western Dance Night or cookie drive, carried a front-page article headlined "If You Prick Us..." (a clever nod to our reading list that year), which in grave tones condemned the use of an offensive term by a new arrival and called for sensitivity to be shown to the school's Jewish students. The authors gallantly spared me from being named directly, "because it is our hope that he did not seek to offend and hurt on purpose, even if he clearly did offend and hurt." Still, my identity as the transgressor in question was hardly a mystery, and the hallways read the verdict on me every day: students and faculty alike gave me a wide berth, as if I were contagious, or violent.

From that point, I cloaked my origins as well as I could. If pressed, I offered a summary statement: *my parents are from the Middle East*, or something equally bland and untraceable. For university I picked a course of study— computer science—that allowed me to disappear into masses of other immigrants and deal with concepts that seemed uncontroversial, like math and algorithms. Still, people often asked me for my opinions, "as an Arab," on touchy topics, mining for the virulence they were sure was underneath my surface. So I spoke carefully, like a diplomat. I learned the beliefs that, like mountains, could not be moved or negotiated, and tried to find within them the crevices where my identity could be acceptable. *Yes, of course Israel, like any other country, has a right to defend itself, but humanitarianism should be considered too, no?* Even this tiptoe felt too disruptive sometimes. If they would let me, I preferred to stay quiet.

Maybe the times have changed, because Firdaos had no interest in any such weak conduct. She had no fear of disapproval.

"Are you *trying* to make people mad?" I asked.

She put her hand to her ear, miming speaking into a telephone. "No, but please hold as I shed a tear for the horrible people who get mad when I call them out."

The summer petered to a close. By September, there were rumours that a reporter had caught wind of the situation at the school and was snooping around. The school dropped their demand for compensation. A few days later, Ms. Warner sent an email to all students and parents, outlining two actions the school would be undertaking: creating an open forum where students could speak to administration and faculty on racial issues, and adding two new electives devoted to the history and challenges of Black and racial- ized communities. Both actions were lifted directly from the list that we and the Taysons had sent to the school.

"EXCUSE ME?" says the second-in-command. "I don't understand what you're saying, Salah."

Romero pumps out messages at top speed in our side chat, but I don't read them.

"I'm saying, Lior, that if you're demanding my future IP, my future ideas and work, then we do not have a deal."

Befuddled by this newly antagonistic, uncollaborative attitude of mine, the second-in-command says he will have to discuss this with his boss. "An impasse like this is above my pay grade," he says.

We have only met his boss, the one I came to think of as the commanding officer, once before, at our kickoff meet- ing. Back then, I had been too shocked to muster much to say, but things are different now.

"Bring him," I say. "Might as well have the decision maker on hand."

With that, I exit the meeting. Romero calls me immediately.

"This is not how a capo acts, capo," he says. "I'm coming over to talk."

"Don't bother. I'm going out. I've had it with them."

I hang up before Romero can respond. My brief and belated display of backbone makes me feel I can show my face to my family. I wander out into the living room.

Marcy is on the sofa, legs tucked underneath her, sobbing as she watches Al Jazeera. There is a news report about air strikes or something. I do not permit myself to absorb it. Instead, I force my attention away from the television and towards my daughter. Firdaos sits cross-legged on the floor, hunched over her phone.

"One hundred eighty-one dead now," she announces without looking up. "Fifty-two are kids. And this is just in the Strip. I can forward you the latest clips if you want."

"No need, I've seen everything," I say, though I've been assiduous in shielding myself. I slump down on the floor next to her. I can hear her laboured breathing. "Are you okay?"

"Half my posts are getting deleted. It's getting to me."

Firdaos had been posting non-stop on her social media accounts for almost a week. She took it upon herself to amplify every atrocity, linking to the people on the ground who reported it, like a second-hand journalist. It was the least she could do, she said. (I didn't tell her this, but hers was one of the first accounts I muted.) Soon she noticed that some of her posts—the more graphic ones, or the ones where her feelings were at their rawest—were being removed almost as soon as she uploaded them. She wasn't the only one.

"They're trying to censor us. It's so obvious. But I have all the time in the world for this. They'll have to hire someone full time just to deal with me."

I do not tell her that there was no need for anyone to be hired, that the biases hard-coded into the algorithms take care of it all without a finger touching a button. I linger near my daughter. The pride I feel in her exacerbates my feelings of duplicity and weakness.

Firdaos senses my eyes. "I'm sorry, do you need your cameras on me or something?"

"No, habeebti. No need."

I can't let my daughter sully herself with BreathCatch any more than she already has.

AS 2021 BEGAN, BreathCatch was on life-support. We had no buyer and no money. We tried some leads for angel investors but were met with scant interest. We applied for some government grants. We explored other development options, like adapting the technology into an exercise app or a security camera. To keep us going, Romero threw in some of his own money in exchange for more equity; it felt almost like charity.

Eventually, one of the federal grant administrators got in touch with us. Off the record, he said that, with so many competitive applications, it was looking unlikely for our tech to be funded by his agency. But, he added, there was one perennially well-funded department that might be interested: National Defence. He connected us with someone there, and we dutifully had a meeting.

Months passed. During this time, Marcy betrayed no view that we sorely needed the stability of a second income. Her steadfast support made me feel more pressure, not less.

Ramadan arrived, and the austerity of its cadences seemed fitting for the emptiness of my life. I dedicated myself to fasting and prayer, making my office a nightly site for solo taraweeh. In the meantime, I trolled job boards. I was surprised when DataHat invited me for an interview, given the sudden, overly enthusiastic way I had quit to start my own business. I met with the same manager I worked under before. He delighted in quizzing me on concepts of application development that he knew I understood well and had used many times while employed there. Still, my interview was late in the afternoon, the hours when the fast renders you sallow-eyed and drained; my responses were not as crisp as they could have been. "So the great start-up dream didn't pan out, did it?" the manager gloated.

At the end of the interview, he smiled and said I should be receiving an email from DataHat soon. The relief on my face must have been obvious, so he added, "Don't get too excited. It will be a no from us. We've had better candidates."

On its own, that should've dumped me into a tailspin of self-pity for months, but the upheaval in Palestine that had started around that time meant I had other things to consume my attention.

Then, on May 9, 2021, on an overcast Sunday morning, our contact at National Defence emailed asking for an urgent call. He said he had a potential buyer for the technology. Would we be interested in receiving an offer?

AS MY WIFE and daughter wallow in the news reports, I feel a desire to purify. I go to wash, put on clean clothes. Places of worship have been ordered closed to curtail transmission of the virus, but some of us have been gathering at noon on Fridays for clandestine jummah prayers in a friend's high-fenced backyard. Brief and safe communion, to help us maintain our sanity. Abdul-Basit's recitation graces my drive there.

I arrive early and park on another street to avoid the neighbours noticing a gathering and calling the police. Some good friends are already here: Rami, Jamal, Husam, others. We greet each other from afar. Seeing them feels like visiting a past life, cool and easy on the heart. The conversation inexorably turns to numbers: COVID, Palestine. No, I cannot do this. I excuse myself, ostensibly to refresh my wudu in the bathroom. I loiter there until I hear that the sermon is about to start.

We have no professional imam among us, so we've devised a rotation for the job. Today our Somali friend Basheer, a construction equipment salesman, is the khatib. There are fewer than a dozen of us in front of him, but his voice quivers from nerves. We sit on prayer mats laid on grass strewn with fallen magnolia flowers. Basheer reads some sentences about forbearance off his cellphone. After a minute, he puts his device down.

He looks to the sky and says, "Ya Allah, may you loosen the knot in my tongue." He looks at us and asks, "How can I speak about anything else?"

With that, everything I have muted this past week comes unmuted in Basheer's voice. The families in Sheikh Jarrah standing their ground as seemingly all of Israel, from politicians to courts to soldiers to settlers, tries to expel them from their homes. The thuds of Gazan buildings levelled by vengeful missiles, the pops of sound bombs as Al-Aqsa is trampled by military boots. The households decimated until only one or two are left carrying the family name. The white phosphorus searing some streets, the skunk water profaning others. The gangs of Israeli citizens running through the streets of Jerusalem, of Lydd, of Haifa, asking people if they are Palestinian, their sticks and guns at the ready.

The guilt of having shielded myself from all this overwhelms me. I fixate on a pink magnolia petal, turn it around with my index finger. I try to notice and memorize everything about it to take me away from what I'm being made to hear. Basheer's point, which he seems to be realizing as he speaks, is that forbearance, in times like these, is not enough.

"Forbearance," he says, "is for things like the pandemic. Stop going to shops for a while, wear protective gear, be patient about your cancelled vacation plans, follow the government guidelines. But for this? Forbearance on its own is not only cowardly; it normalizes what should not be normal. It makes you part of the problem."

Basheer asks: "So what should we be doing, then?"

I do not wait for his answer. No one just leaves a jummah prayer, but I do.

In the car I silence Abdul-Basit. Having regained control of my surroundings, I talk myself into resenting Basheer.

God does not burden us with what we don't have the strength to bear, Basheer. You do not know what I am already bearing, Basheer. You are not teetering on the brink like I am, Basheer. And who are you to expound on politics in the first place, Basheer? In times like these, a professional imam would have known to focus on religion, to sanitize his speech of polemics that get us all into trouble, Basheer.

It is comforting to separate yourself. Why should we obsess about problems that are so far away? It's sunny here; it's spring. There are magnolia petals. It's all fine.

When I arrive home, I am calmer. My head is back on straight. I text Romero. *Sorry, bud. I know I didn't act right. But I'm ready to resume the negotiations now.*

Never mind, he texts back. *They said we can pick it up tomorrow. The boss isn't going to just show up to give you a pep talk anytime you have a nervous breakdown.*

It's late afternoon, which means it's nighttime in Palestine. That's when the Israelis redouble their bombings. The videos on TV are like a light and sound show. But at least the footage of the bloodied faces and bodies will not emerge until morning. It is a respite for the house, of sorts.

In the living room, Firdaos is still on the floor. She looks even more agitated than before. Her wheezing is audible.

"What are you doing?" I ask.

"Getting clobbered, it seems."

Firdaos tells me that her posts—the ones that were not deleted—have been getting attention at school. Some of her friends sent her private messages of timid support, or asked her to clarify what was going on because they didn't quite get it. Others, including some parents of kids at her school, posted replies contradicting Firdaos and suggesting she educate herself. They sent her news articles from Western media that gave the impression that the violence was equal between the two sides and instigated by the Palestinians. As Firdaos continued to post, the reactions became more aggressive and sometimes threatening. Firdaos, defiant, responded to each one.

You are wrong and racist. Sorry for you.

Then, just now, someone alerted Firdaos that she had been listed on a website that billed itself as a directory of anti-Semitic high school and college students across North America. On the site, Firdaos found several pages dedicated to her, all created in the last few days. They published her full name, several of her pictures from social media (including one from when she was twelve years old), the name of our neighbourhood in Toronto, the name of her school, and a long write-up of the offensive acts Firdaos had engaged in online, with quotes taken from her posts. The page noted that Firdaos's online presence frequently features a picture of Fatima Bernawi, *a renowned Arab terrorist who tried to bomb a Jewish cinema (click here to learn more). It is obvious that this student is in favour of terrorism against Jewish people and the State of Israel.*

"I can't believe a website like this exists," I muster.

"Believe it, baba. And, bonus: it looks like this page has been forwarded to the principal at my school."

I STILL BLAME my failure to reject the offer for BreathCatch on the way they sent it to us. It arrived late at night, two days before Eid, in an email from the attorney for the interested party. That party asked to remain anonymous until the execution of a mutual NDA. What the email did disclose was an astounding purchase price.

For seven or eight hours, that email was the victory of my lifetime. Romero and I feasted our eyes on it dozens of times, pumping our fists until our creaky shoulders ached. We wondered what this secretive government agency could want with our software, what plans might they have? And the mystery of it all only heightened our delight. Before going to bed, I printed the email, smoothed the paper that I had snatched too excitedly from the printer, and scrawled a note on top of it.

It's a day early, but Eid Mubarak, habeebti. Thank you for always believing in me.

I left the paper on Marcy's nightstand, making it the second most beautiful thing in that room, after my wife's gentle snores.

The next morning, I prepared to attend a meeting with the buyer, which felt like a bonus Eid before the Eid. With our lawyer present as well, Romero and I sat up straight as rods, our smiles dumb and infinite, as we waited for the secure video connection to reveal our new benefactors. The screens resolved into pictures, and we saw the tiles. One of them showed a dingy government office, where the man I came to think of as the second-in-command sat at a desk. Another tile showed a rooftop location, where an older man sat on a lawn chair, behind him a vista of hills strewn with trees and stone houses. Near him was a flagpole that bore a fluttering piece of fabric on which I could see Israel's familiar six-pointed star between two blue stripes.

The image was so shocking that for a moment I wondered if my computer had by accident picked up an errant satellite signal, or a YouTube video that Firdaos was hate-watching. The man on the rooftop, the one I came to think of as the commanding officer, began to address us in a light European accent.

"We at the Israeli Ministry of Defense are admirers of your technology, gentlemen. We are happy that you have decided to speak to us to see if we are a good fit. There is a great tradition of co-operation between our two countries in many areas. Hopefully, this will be just the latest example."

It took me a moment to realize that, in referring to my country, he meant Canada.

"I understand that your technology was originally developed for medical purposes," he continued. "We can see how it might be helpful there, and should we complete the purchase, we may choose to use it in our hospitals in the future. However, what attracted us is that the technology is useful in cases when a person's face is partially or fully obstructed. My colleague Lior here tells me you've tested it with patients wearing medical masks? As you know, we are facing threats every day from masked persons. Terrorists slingshot rocks and explosives at our soldiers, who are just boys and girls doing their jobs: defending Israel and keeping her citizens safe. The terrorists can act with complete impunity because we cannot readily identify them. Instead, we have to resort to manhunts, interrogations, close inspections of video footage, and so forth. Your technology has the potential to simplify all of that. With it, we can compile a breath database, which we would then mine for matches to the criminals hiding in their scarves. We could install the technology on street corners, on drones, or on helmets; we could even have our covert units use it with their personal phones. The potential is really exciting for us. Okay, let me now turn it over to Lior, who is the person who really knows everything here. He can talk about how we would like to proceed with this transaction."

The rest of that first meeting went by in a blur. On the break we took later, Romero summarized the major points for me. The Israelis would like to move very quickly, because budgets were particularly loose during times of heightened armed conflict like the one currently taking place. They estimated there was a week left in the hostilities (I winced at how confidently they provided that estimate), so everything had to be buttoned down very soon. We would risk getting deprioritized if we waited too long, as there were several other technologies they were considering.

"So what do you say, capo? All good?"

I didn't answer. Instead, I locked my screen and staggered to the bathroom upstairs, frantically trying to think of ways to reject the offer. I saw Marcy, coming out of the bedroom. In her hand she had the paper I had left on her nightstand. One of her cheeks was red and creased from sleep. Her mouth hung open in confusion. "Is this real?" she asked.

I wanted to nullify the note somehow before it had stabilized in my wife's head. I could say it was a prank or a hacker or something.

"Is this real, Salah?" she asked again. This time a faint expectant smile appeared on her face. The way she said my name — properly pronouncing the Arabic letters "sawd" at its beginning and "ha" at its end, like my mother showed her—never failed to arrest me.

It might seem strange that I didn't agonize more over my response. But I was broke, couldn't even get my old, terrible job back, and Romero would have flipped figurative tables if I refused to sell and let him reap the rewards. Really, though, it came down to this: I didn't have the stomach to disappoint Marcy.

"Yes," I said. "It's real."

Marcy padded towards me. "Salah. Salah. Salah..." Then she drew closer and hugged me. "I'm so proud of you."

It felt surreal to be trudging back to my office with the answer I was about to give.

"Surprised to see you back so soon, gentlemen," said the commanding officer. Do you have any questions that we can help you with?"

"No, we do not," I answered. "We will go ahead with the transaction."

"Just like that? We're ready for takeoff?" The commanding officer arched his eyebrow.

"Yes."

"Khalas!" he said, throwing a common Arabic word at me in what felt like mocking recognition. "Yalla, let's get this work started!"

On some idiotic level, I had thought that if I made the decision quickly—if I instantly transformed a present choice into a past choice—then that would be the end of it. Instead, every minute in the week that followed was laced with the acid of that decision coming back up through my esophagus, over and over.

The first day was the worst. I felt like I had personally caused what was happening in Palestine. Every time someone was arrested, it was like I was the one who dragged them by their collars and handed them to the enemy, who then hurled them to the ground, suffocated them with a knee on their necks, and threw them to rot in jail, or in a grave.

Take them, they are the ones, I know them by their very breath.

I constantly searched for a pretext to undo the deal. Eventually, I couldn't help but tell Romero.

"You know we're basically giving them a licence to go after my own people, right?"

"I don't like where you're going with this, capo," he said. "Look, we did not make a gun. We did not make a missile. We did not make anything that hurts people. Total opposite! We made something for medical use. They want to use it for something else, that's on them."

"Is it nice to pretend to be that stupid?"

"Another thing: Do you think if we don't sell to them, they'll just say, 'Oh, too bad, we'll give up and go home?' No! They'll go ahead and make something like it themselves. How long do you think it would take them?"

"Sure, but at least then I wouldn't have to be involved."

"But you're not involved! You're just taking their money."

Romero did not understand this sudden appearance of a conscience on my part. I couldn't blame him. I had cloaked myself so well that these new questions seemed irreconcilable with the person I had presented myself as before. But I asked them anyway, hoping in vain that the theatre of doing so could exonerate me.

"They're going to kill people like me, like my daughter," I said. "People just trying to keep their homes, their land."

"But that's where you're wrong. They're not going after people like you. They're going after people who target *them*."

"My God," I replied. "If I were there, I might be doing that, too."

"But you're not there, you're here. It's a big difference, capo."

I GO TO my office and close the door. I frantically run searches to try to find out who is behind the website that has published Firdaos's information. I am not sure what our legal rights are, but there has to be a way to get them to take the information down. She is just a child. There have to be limits to this warfare against us, no?

Before I get anywhere, my phone rings. It's Ms. Warner, the principal. I've become far too familiar with that woman.

"Sir, I regret to have to be contacting you again" is how she starts. This time, Ms. Warner is not treading carefully. Her voice is self-righteous, her sentences direct. "Your daughter has been posting some controversial things online. Are you aware of this?"

"I am aware she's been online a lot, yes. I understand it's common with teenagers."

Ms. Warner does not appreciate my glibness. She informs me of the pile of complaints that she has received about Firdaos, and the deep hurt and trauma that these complaints describe. She informs me that some of Firdaos's trauma-inducing activities have even been perpetrated during times she is supposed to be in virtual classes. But what is most upsetting—and Ms. Warner can hardly believe she is saying these words about one of her students—is that Firdaos has put up an image of a well-known terrorist on her school email account. Firdaos's classmates are forced to look at that image every day when they email or message her, when they look at the class list, or when they're in a virtual classroom with her. How could these students help but feel incredibly unsafe? Some of them were even tricked into thinking this terrorist is an admirable figure—a civil rights leader or something—and started using the picture themselves. The school is sympathetic to the pressure Firdaos is under, given the toll her disease takes, but racist hostility and disinformation of the kind she's peddling will never be acceptable.

"And if I may remind you," Ms. Warner adds, "this is not the first time that your daughter has caused a major disruption at our school."

"Well, but, if I recall correctly, we landed on last time being okay in the end, didn't we?"

Ms. Warner ignores what I said. Instead, she gives me an ultimatum. Firdaos is to take the Bernawi picture down immediately, along with her more reckless posts on social media. Firdaos is to also write an apology in the school paper expressing her remorse and committing to educating and bettering herself. If Firdaos doesn't do these things, Ms. Warner will suspend her, or worse.

"Sir, our school has always been committed to ending racism in all its forms. And yet, because of your daughter's actions, our good name is on an anti-Semitism watch list. I have to treat this like the emergency it is."

I tell Ms. Warner that I will think about her offer.

"It's not an offer. And think about it fast. I'm not going to let this fester past tomorrow." With that, she hangs up.

I understand Ms. Warner's position. I understand how Firdaos's actions look. Our world — *this* world, this neighbourhood, this school, this country, this continent, this system — is not set up for someone like Firdaos to speak up. The rejection of what Firdaos stands for is so innate as to be a reflex, one that does not need to be further analyzed or justified. I find it easier to think of it mathematically — it's like dividing by zero. Why can't it be done? Because it cannot. It doesn't compute, has never computed, and will never compute. The illegality of it is absolute. No one would flinch if Firdaos was suspended. Only a suspension? they would wonder. That's what kids who deface the bathroom stalls get. Unless she repents, she should be punished even more harshly.

But getting suspended *would* be disastrous for my daughter. Next year she will be submitting university applications. A black mark like that is very hard to recover from. And for what? For the chance to stand in front of a raging bulldozer?

I go looking for Marcy. She is out in the backyard, tending to the tomato beds, searching for the tiny green pellets of fruit. Marcy has been spending most of her time either on her phone, organizing aid campaigns, or in the company of her plants trying to escape the news amid the fragrance from her thicket of unstoppable mint.

I recount to her my conversation with the principal. Marcy sighs. She does not stop running her hands through the soil, snatching out weeds.

"I knew it would be something like this," she says. "I've been dodging Warner's calls."

"Why would you do that?"

"To buy time? I guess I don't want to tell Firdaos to stop."

"Are you insane?"

"I'm not—at least I don't think I am. But I don't know how I can ask our daughter to witness what she's witnessing and keep her mouth shut. The girl has to be allowed to breathe, Salah. We all do."

It is clear to me that the situation has driven Marcy outside the realm of rational thought. It doesn't seem to matter to her that you cannot divide by zero. It's up to me to protect both her and Firdaos.

I leave Marcy in the yard and find Firdaos at the dining table, still immersed in her phone. Her nose is red, and the rims of her eyes look freshly wiped and tender. Her breathing is laboured.

I don't quite have the right words figured out, so I just say hey.

Firdaos sniffs and looks up at me, musters her usual sardonic smile. "So, new developments. Looks like I'm going to be suspended. Principal just sent me an email. She's fantasizing that I might take down the Bernawi picture and apologize for it."

I recognize this is a moment when what I say to my daughter could affect our relationship for a long time. Still, I have to be clear-minded for both of us.

"Habeebti, please, the fact is this will not go well for us."

"Why?"

"Because the majority of people don't think like we think. They don't experience what we experience, and they don't know the truth like we do."

"You're wrong. Adie understands. So do many of my friends."

"Has Adie been posting like you?"

"All the time."

"Show me."

Firdaos searches Adie's profiles but can't find anything. Then she says that Adie usually just posts stories, which disappear after a while. Firdaos searches her picture roll, and finds screen caps of some of them. (I feel a pang of sadness at the thought that my daughter so wanted to treasure her friend's support that she made sure to capture it before it vanished.) The few she digs up are of laconic posts asking, in a general way, for the violence to stop, with emojis of crying or pleading.

Firdaos looks sheepish. "It's not her fault," she says. "Adie doesn't fully understand what's going on."

"That's the point, isn't it?"

"Whatever. Just because I'm alone in this doesn't mean I'm wrong," says Firdaos.

"Please, habeebti."

"Please *you*, baba. It's not enough that the social media companies are deleting my posts, now I have to delete them myself? Are you *all* trying to break me?"

Firdaos and I talk in circles. She looks away as I speak. Her body shrinks from me when I try to touch her.

My phone vibrates. It's Romero. *Great news. Lior says they can meet with us again tonight at* II. *The boss will be there. Our lawyer says he can make it, too. Be ready to make nice, capo.*

OK, I respond. Firdaos takes the opportunity of my typing those two letters to leave.

For dinner, Marcy makes bamia, a dish of stewed okra that she learned from my mother. It is a meal that I hate, in all its oozy depravity, and it is perfect for today. I eat it in silence. I scoop two more helpings for myself after I'm done the first. Firdaos eats nothing but plain rice, to which Marcy does not raise any objection. The only sound is the syncopated hissing of the evening sprinklers outside.

After Firdaos and Marcy have gone to bed, I try to untangle my anxiety about Firdaos from my anxiety about what might come in the negotiations tonight. I can barely remember the reason why I stopped the negotiations in the first place. It feels impossible to understand what side I am on, or what I am prepared to stand for.

When the video conference reveals Lior and his boss again, I don't even think of escaping, not anymore. Lior invites the commanding officer, addressing him as Yosef, to speak. At first Yosef's head fills the screen, the dots of his stubble appearing in intimate detail. He says a few words of greeting, then adjusts his camera so he is not so close.

Yosef is once again on his rooftop. The breeze renders his thin silver hair into a nimbus around his head. The hilly scenery behind him is bathed in the pinks of dawn. *His* dawn.

Yosef jokes that he is not overjoyed to have been dragged out of bed for a deal that should have been concluded very easily. It's a holiday where he lives, and his wife will not like that he's working.

"But business is business," he says. "I'm told the current problem is your future IP, correct?"

Really, it is no longer a problem for me. The only position that feels natural to me now is submission. I open my mouth to say as much, but Yosef keeps talking.

"Well, let's take that off the table, then, Salah. We can live without your future IP. Mind, this is something most inventors have no trouble giving us at the amounts we are paying. But there is always an emotional element with these things, isn't there? So, we concede on this point. We will run with the technology ourselves once we have it."

Incredible, capo, messages Romero. *Big victory for you on this one!* He is not aware that he doesn't need to persuade me anymore.

"Thanks for this concession," I say to Yosef.

"Okay, good. But, listen, in exchange, can you agree to assist us with your tech whenever we need it over the next twenty-four months? The code is complicated, and we'd rather not waste our time figuring out how something works if we can just call you. Make sense?"

It makes sense, but I hate it. It means I'm tied to them for a while still, a nursemaid for their new addition.

"Twelve months," I say, "And billed at my hourly rate."

Yosef agrees quickly.

"Wow, capo, wow," says Romero. But he is *not* on mute. His comment that was intended solely for me has been blurted out for everyone on the video call to hear. He begins to apologize, but Yosef interrupts him. "What did you say? Kapo? What do you mean by that?"

"Nothing," Romero says. "It's just something I call Salah, like a joke between us. Because he's the captain of our company. It's an Italian word."

"I see," says Yosef. "Because it's a very bad word for Jews. In the Nazi camps, some Jews were put in charge of other Jews, usually to torture them and make them work harder. They called them the kapos, and they were given privileges over the rest. The kapos were brutal, as bad as the Nazis, maybe worse. These days if you want to really tar a Jew, just call him a kapo. It's the same as saying traitor."

"That's horrible," says Romero. "That's not what I meant at all."

"I would hope not!" Yosef says with a laugh. "But, between us, I can't imagine what it was like to be in the shoes of a kapo back in those times. They had the Nazis at their throats. Who knows what that level of extreme desperation and danger might lead a person to do... I suppose it's a good reminder of why we're all here today, isn't it? To make sure that sort of situation never happens again to the Jewish people. Shall we continue?"

"Let's," I say.

The rest of the meeting proceeds in the same way: Yosef plowing through provisions with purpose, me conceding with little resistance. Around four a.m., we are done, my digital signature the final touch on the contract.

I am much, much richer than I ever imagined.

The house is quiet with the sleep of my family. The betrayal I have perpetrated, noiseless. I look around my living room. It will soon be a different room, in a better house. There are infinity pools in my future, and likely a sauna too, but my main thought is to never let my family know what I did.

I wait for dawn so I can perform the morning prayer. I peer through the slightly open door of Firdaos's room. I hope that today my daughter might rise and join me, like she used to as a child.

I linger, but she does not wake up. She is very still in her bed.

I wash, I pray, I turn to sleep.

I WAKE TO the sound of lawn mowers buzzing, chains being pulled.

The events of the last day come to me in gradual, painful progression. When Firdaos crosses my mind, I panic. She still needs to take down her profile picture. I look at the time: 2:30 p.m. Still groggy, I stumble through the house, searching for Firdaos. For Marcy.

I have to call Ms. Warner to buy more time. I don't know what I will say, but I dial anyway.

"Hello, Salah," Ms. Warner says. "Thank you for your efforts with your daughter. I'm sure it wasn't easy."

"No, it hasn't been. But we're making progress. I'm sure that by Monday this will all be sorted out."

"I'm sorry? What more were you planning to do?"

"I'm not following, Ms. Warner."

"Well, Firdaos has already taken down the picture and the posts, and apologized. What more is there? I suppose if you wanted to make a donation in her name..."

"Wait, she has done all that?"

"Yes, she even said you were her inspiration."

I hang up and look up Firdaos's social media accounts.

I don't see anything at first, but then I remember I have to unmute her. Now I see Firdaos's profile picture has been taken down and replaced by an Israeli flag. There is a new post, dated a few hours ago. My mind scatters.

I drift to my office. The sun is flooding through its large windows. In her post, my daughter said this is where she spent her morning. I try to retrace her steps. Maybe she came here for the sunlight. Maybe, in spite of our disagreements, or because of them, she wanted to feel closer to me. She sat at my desk. But the computer screen is locked, like always, and my password is strong. Maybe she rooted in the drawers and wastebasket—but there was nothing for her to find.

But look.

On the floor, there is a package in a manila envelope. I've never seen this package before. Firdaos must have opened the package, like I am opening it now. She must have read the first few pages, like I am reading. That's when she dropped it and wrote her social media post, the one with a voice that was somehow both incensed and defeated. The social media post in which she said she felt like a hypo-crite to be taking a stand for her people in Palestine while her family in Toronto profits off their suffering. The social media post in which she tagged all her classmates, and everyone we know, all our friends and relatives.

I call Marcy; I call Firdaos. Neither answers.

I check my texts. The only new messages are from Romero, two of them.

Couldn't sleep, too excited. I printed the signed contract and dropped it off for you. Hoped to see you, but your daughter said you were sleeping. I just want to say that I know the process was hard for you, but you came through like a champ in the end.

Time to enjoy your life, capo.

ACKNOWLEDGEMENTS

These stories engage a people who have been violently and unjustly dispossessed of their land. I wrote them while living on the land of other people who were also violently and unjustly dispossessed. I acknowledge that land as the traditional territory of the Anishinabeg, the Wendat, the Haudenosaunee, and the Mississaugas of the Credit. I am thankful to all of them.

I am deeply grateful to my brilliant editor, Shirarose Wilensky, for her courage in unhesitatingly seeking and championing this collection, and for her grace, perspicacity, and deft hand through the editorial process. My debt to her is great.

Many thanks to: everyone at House of Anansi who helped steer this book to publication, including especially Michelle MacAleese, Alysia Shewchuk, Debby de Groot,

237

and Karen Brochu; Emilia Morgan for her editorial support; and my agent, Stephanie Sinclair at CookeMcDermid.

Thanks to the Canada Council for the Arts and the distinguished judges of the 2021 CBC Short Story Prize: Souvankham Thammavongsa, Craig Davidson, and the late Lee Maracle.

Thanks to the University of Toronto School of Continuing Studies, and especially to Dennis Bock and Michel Basilières.

For their important feedback and support, thanks to the readers of early drafts of my stories, chief among them Basel Teebi, Leslie Carlin, Diana Catargiu, Sam Conover, Adam Fiske, Valentina Khanzina, Janelle Taylor, Benno Tutter, Margaret Watson, and Sophia Wen. For their valuable support and discussions, thanks to Arun Krishnamurti and Salma Hussain. For the strand of inspiration that led to "Woodland," thanks once again to Margaret Watson, and, for linguistic assistance with that story, thanks to Sara Benbrahim.

Thanks to Farzana Doctor, Sahar Mustafa, Hasan Namir, Danny Ramadan, Rebecca Sacks, Nyla Matuk, and Ayelet Tsabari for their generous review and comments.

Special thanks to Geraldine Baker, one of the earliest supporters of my writing. In the many years when I did not write a word, I thought of her words.

Acknowledgements

The title of "The Reflected Sky" is from the opening stanza of Shade's poem in *Pale Fire* by Vladimir Nabokov.

The epigraph is excerpted from a poem composed in 1971 by my late father, Dr. Ahmad S. Teebi. My love and thanks to him, and to my mother, Amal Qudsi. Their shadows loom over everything I write.

So much love to Leith and Dalia. Finally, to Hala: this book would not have happened without you.

SAEED TEEBI is a writer and lawyer based in Toronto. His story "Her First Palestinian" was shortlisted for the 2021 CBC Short Story Prize. He was born to Palestinian parents in Kuwait and has lived in Canada since 1993.